"Where are those nerves of steel now, Fairlie?"

She glanced behind her to see that she was running out of space. "I'd be afraid of any man who had the Tate organization behind him."

"Forget the company. You're afraid of me."

Then he kissed her with a sweet intimacy that should have surprised her but didn't. She said his name, and there was pleasure and awe in her voice.

"Now we know," he murmured, loosening his hold on her. "The feeling is mutual."

Carson Tate always got what he wanted. He wanted the house. He wanted her, too. And she was making it easy for him.

"You caught me off guard," she snapped. "But I'm not about to lose my head over mere technique."

But the smug smile remained on his face. "And I thought we'd reached an understanding."

ANN
CHARLTON

an irresistible force

Harlequin Books

TORONTO • NEW YORK • LONDON
AMSTERDAM • PARIS • SYDNEY • HAMBURG
STOCKHOLM • ATHENS • TOKYO • MILAN

Harlequin Presents first edition February 1986
ISBN 0-373-10857-5

Original hardcover edition published in 1985
by Mills & Boon Limited

Printed in U.S.A.

CHAPTER ONE

FAIRLIE was shocked. She knew what to expect but she was shocked anyway. The weatherboard cottage looked smaller than she remembered. It teetered on its Queensland stilts like an old circus performer shaky after years of sureness. Its whimsical verandah, swollen into a rotunda-like shape at one end, seemed less spacious, its windows shrunken and defensive. Even the garden, bounded by a fence that lacked a slat here and there, was oddly spare.

When she had paid the cab driver, Fairlie stood by her luggage on the pavement and viewed Nan's house properly. It had always seemed so large to her as a child—niched and crannied as only an old house could be, full of delightful corners and cubby houses in the dim spaces beneath the house stumps. Once, when she was eleven, she had spent her whole summer holidays here ... the fourteen year old images persisted ... sparkling white painted lattice work slanting mosaics of sunlight across the floor beneath the house, Pa's dahlias tied to stakes in the front garden, Nan's tomatoes tied to stakes out the back. The mango tree which smelled of the fruit at the merest snap of a twig. Sun and insect buzz and the aggrieved clok-clok of chickens ... Nan's washing trolley trundling another load of whiter than white to the clothes line. Dear Nan ...

The air trembled. One of the massive earthmovers roared as Fairlie picked up her bags and began to walk to the house. Dust flew and she turned away momentarily as the breeze blew it in her face. When she moved forward again, the orange monster was rounding the corner by Nan's gates. It stopped, close against the fence, half over the dirt encrusted pavement that was riddled with its tracks.

'Could you move, please?' Fairlie looked up at the driver as he turned off the machine and gave every impression of leaving it parked there only inches parallel to the gate, barring access to the house. He was wearing earpads and pointed at them, spreading his hands with a shrug when he reached the ground. Then with an insolent grin he began to walk away.

Fairlie put her suitcases down. So it was every bit as bad as Aunt Leila had told her. Worse. Another machine was working on the gaping hole that had been the homes of two of Nan's neighbours and there were several men working on the land that ran behind her back fence. The Reynolds house on the other side was now just a flattened mish-mash of mouldings and memories. And beyond the devastation that surrounded Nan's cottage, commercial steel and glass frowned down on the tiny remnant of suburbia.

Fairlie went after the sauntering driver. He swung around when she tapped him on the shoulder. She reached out and dislodged his earpads. 'Move your machine please.'

He grinned. 'I'm off now. Smoko time.'

'Do you always leave the key in it when you stop for smoko? I'm sure the foreman wouldn't like that. Or Mr Tate.'

At the mention of the Colossus Constructions top man, the driver merely laughed. 'Oooh, namedropper.,' he mocked. 'What's it to you anyway?'

'I want to use the gate,' she told him. 'Now.'

'You've got good long legs,' he gave them a comprehensive look. 'You'll be able to climb over the old girl's fence all right.'

Fairlie's lips tightened. So that was how it was. She turned on her heel and the man guffawed with his mates. 'That skirt might be a bit tight for climbing, darlin'——' he shouted. 'We'll stick around for the show.'

This might not be a good idea, she thought as she stopped beside the earthmover, her hands on her hips. Even the tyres were taller than she was.

'Goin' for a spin in Old Ripper, darlin'?' the driver called. 'Mind now, she's a real devil in reverse!'

Their guffaws stopped though when she hitched up her skirt and climbed in to the seat.

Suddenly she was high, looking down on the startled men. So surprised were they that they didn't move until she turned the ignition key. Then there was a lot of activity and cries of male outrage and she thought the driver bellowed something about 'a quarter of a million dollars', but Old Ripper was roaring and she discovered why the man had been wearing earpads. He was absolutely right. Ripper *was* a devil in reverse and Fairlie couldn't find a forward gear. She was heading back towards the excavations at a fair speed, scattering the workmen. Then she found the brake. Old Ripper jolted to a stop, engine protesting mightily. The driver scrambled up and reached over for the ignition.

'Oh no you don't,' Fairlie yelled, 'not yet,' and set off again in reverse. The man's cursing would have burned her ears off had they not already been assaulted by the machine's noise—he grabbed the gear knob and changed into forward. Nan's fence loomed up and Fairlie stamped on the brake. She switched off and while the driver wiped his ashen brow, removed the keys and dropped them into her pocket.

'Isn't it quiet?' she volunteered as he fixed her with a baleful stare. Inside she was shaking like a leaf but she pulled up her skirt and descended from Old Ripper as composedly as she could. The men weren't, she noticed with satisfaction, awfully interested in her legs anymore. They looked amazed, angry—relieved. Well, at least they knew she meant business. She might not have arrived with bugles blowing, but the cavalry was here. She patted Old Ripper in mock affection. 'She *is* a devil, isn't she?' she smiled. 'Don't leave her parked across our gates again or I'll have to take her for another spin.'

'Next time,' the driver sneered, still pale and shaking, 'I won't leave the key in it.'

'In that case I'll have her towed away under Council Ordinance twenty-four.' The man frowned. 'I *can* do it,' she assured him, wondering if there was any such thing as Ordinance twenty-four. 'In future you'll have me to contend with, not one frightened widow in her seventies who just wants to go on living in her own house.' They were silent as she walked away and the driver belatedly noticed the missing keys. 'Hey,' he yelled.

'Oh yes——' Fairlie turned around and slipped a hand into her pocket. 'Your keys. Here—catch.' She drew back her arm and the sun gleamed on the object that arced high over the men's heads to drop into the excavations beyond.

Nan was at the gate, fumbling with the catch, her delight at Fairlie's arrival and her distress at the scene jumbling her greetings.

'Oh, my dear girl—Fairlie my darling—so direct, so

brave just like your mother. How did you know how to drive that thing?'

Fairlie hugged her. Her grandmother seemed more fragile, less steady than she remembered.

'Nan, I didn't have a clue. I'm lucky to be alive. But I thought they needed a bit of a shake up. Insolent devils.' Fairlie glared over at the group of men searching for the keys. Old Ripper remained docilely where she'd left her.

She glanced up at the building that flanked the site. It was small by Colossus standards. And conservative. Most of the Company's sites sprouted bronze reflective towers or circular giants. This was of course, but the beginning of the development. Given time it would become part of a complex as eyecatching as any of Colossus' projects. Given time—and Nan's land. It really was amazing that Mr Tate of the shrewd 'takeover Tates' should have been caught out like this. Fairlie could not believe that they were beginning work before they'd actually bought up this last small patch of green. But then, they had ways of 'persuading' the last reluctant householder to sell out.

Near the top of the Colossus building the gleaming chequered pattern of windows was broken by a bronzed strip. There were faint outlines of foliage against the glass there as if the floor was some kind of conservatory.

'I wonder if Mr Tate himself has an office up there,' Fairlie murmured as she picked up her luggage.

'Yes dear, I believe he has.' Nan took her cabin bag and they went through the smaller of the two gates that used to be Pa's car access.

She smiled nervously at Fairlie. 'The keys dear—do you think you should have thrown them away like that?'

They walked up the steep front stairs, looking across at the site. The workmen were still scrabbling about in the dirt, searching. Their smoko was not proving restful.

'I'm sure they have spares. But I hope the foreman blasts that driver for losing his,' Fairlie said without remorse. She grinned as they paused on the worn timber verandah. 'Anyway all they're like to find there is a twenty cent piece.' Fairlie put her bags down in the polished hall and took the keys from her pocket.

'Fairlie, you *kept* them!' For a moment Nan looked anxious at the idea of flouting the men with the mighty machines, then she laughed. 'You're a terror, dear. What will you do with them?'

'Oh, I don't know yet. I might decide on guerrilla tactics—you know, get up at two in the morning and shift Old Ripper to new pastures. Hold her to ransom even.' Nan looked horrified. 'Just kidding Nan. Even I wouldn't do that.'

But Fairlie's jokes and her small strike back at Colossus had lifted Nan's spirits. The lines of anxiety relaxed on her brow.

'It's so good to have you here,' she said.

'It's good to be here. Even if half the neighbourhood has been wrecked.' From one kind of disaster to another. She thought of the wreckage she'd left behind in Melbourne. Broken promises, broken engagement, broken heart . . . well, maybe that was going too far. Hearts like hers didn't break under stress. They toughened up, hardened, learned the lesson well. Hearts like hers didn't make the same mistake twice. All the same it was a relief to have left the city that held so much of Ben. Even hearts like hers needed time to toughen. More time than she'd thought.

She took her bags into a small, high ceilinged room

furnished with a cedar bed and matching wardrobe and dressing table. One of Nan's superb crocheted bedspreads covered the bed and on the tiny table beside it was the same porcelain vase with its delicate rose pattern that she remembered from that summer. It was touchingly full of fern fronds—not the flowers that used to abound in the garden when Pa was alive.

'Did you bring your paintings dear?' Nan asked as Fairlie unzipped a bag and set out a few essentials.

'The ones for the exhibition are going direct to the gallery,' she said, 'and I've got a few you might like, packed in the crates that should arrive here soon.'

'That's lovely. You do such wonderful work. Talented like your father.' But she saw the look on Fairlie's face and didn't pursue that. Instead she made tea in her brown crockery pot and produced gem scones that brought out the eleven-year-old in Fairlie. Gobbling down three, she smiled sheepishly. 'I can see I'll have to be careful Nan. Your cooking could transform me into a tub.' She patted her flat stomach and smoothed down the navy linen skirt. Her jacket hung over the back of the wooden kitchen chair and she had rolled up the sleeves of her white silk shirt that she wore with a navy and red tie.

'You're too thin,' Nan clucked. 'Have another scone dear.'

Fairlie obliged, amused as Nan went on to relate her theory of good health and a 'decent covering of flesh' going hand in hand. Thinness to her was a sign of neglect on someone's part—as she told Fairlie again now.

'You're a lovely girl——' she began and hesitated, her eyes wandering over the rather severe clothes that Fairlie liked to wear for business or travelling. They weren't Nan's idea of femininity it was clear. Fairlie grinned. Nan wouldn't much care for her painting garb either.

As a painter Fairlie was messy—her clothes were splotched with brush wipes, with inadvertent sprays and paint dribbles and if it was possible to earn her living from painting she would probably spend most of her time dressed in jeans, overalls and outsized shirts. But it wasn't possible. Materials and training were too costly and not offset by the occasional sales of her work. Fortunately, hand in hand with her art training she had learned secretarial skills and once past the age of dreamy visions of a studio and painting full-time, she put her typing and business studies to use. She had made a remarkable discovery on entering what she anticipated would be a boring bread-and-butter job. She liked it. The disciplines of business life had a certain appeal—in some odd way to her, they paralleled the disciplines of art, though she had a tough job ever explaining that to anyone else. To Ben she had been a puzzle. He had seen her often enough, oblivious to her surroundings, overalled, face paint-smudged and her hair in an uncontrollable honey blonde mass—and just as often tailored and alert, hair drawn back to a smooth, fettered knob as it was now . . . the artist and the secretary. Ben had always been intrigued by the contrasting images of her. But not intrigued enough.

'. . . so like your mother. The same greeny-blue eyes.' Nan smiled reminiscently at Fairlie. The old lady was very tactfully getting around to what she wanted to say. 'Felicity used to look just beautiful in frills.'

Fairlie's mouth twitched. 'Frills, Nan?'

'Yes, you know—*feminine* clothes——' she tried hard not to look at Fairlie's tie, '—and her hair—just like yours it was. It always looked lovely loose.'

'Hmm. I daren't let mine out too often. It runs wild. What do you think of my tie and shirt? I bought them when I was in Paris.' Paris and the tie and shirt were B.B. Before Ben.

'Oh, Paris.' Nan pursed her lips. 'Yes, they always have such—unusual clothes, don't they? More tea dear?'

Over the remainder of the gem scones Nan chatted about the far-flung members of the family but Fairlie noticed the ceaseless fidgeting of her hand on the table, the twisting of her wafer-thin wedding ring with her thumb.

'Nan, you'd better tell me the whole story,' she said, putting out a hand to stay the old woman's anxiety.

It was simple really. The creeping changes in the near city suburbs had reached Nan. For the last decade the city's steel had spread through Spring Hill towards this street. Those who lived here had not been unduly alarmed at the new skyline of cranes and towers. Sad perhaps, but not alarmed. After all who would want to build offices in *their* street, on *their* land? But old Mr Ellis had died at ninety-two and his house was sold by his heirs and soon old Mr Ellis' place was marked by an office block and a car park. So it was not long before the house next to it was up for sale and when the neighbours got to thinking about another big building throwing them into the shade most of the day, another house and another was sold.

'When the Reynolds said they were selling out, I was so upset and then those men came to see me . . .'

'What men?'

Nan's thumb pushed at her wedding ring. 'Oh, I don't remember their names. I didn't like them much. They asked me if I wanted to sell the house and at first I said no. Then they said that there would be no neighbours and big offices all around and it sounded so dreadful that I said yes——'

'Nan, you told them you *would* sell? Did you sign anything?'

'No. It was a long time before anyone brought me papers to sign and by then I knew I didn't want to leave even if they built a skyscraper next door——'

'Did they pressure you?'

'Oh no. They didn't make threats or anything, Fairlie. But oh, it does seem selfish of me I suppose, wanting to stay on here when all those men's jobs depend on them starting the rest of the project. I don't like to think of putting men out of work,' she shook her head, 'men with wives and children. I'd feel responsible. And you can't stand in the way of progress . . .'

Fairlie snorted. 'Rubbish. They're not contractors, they're Colossus' own staff. If this job is delayed they'll work on another one. That kind of psychological hogwash is almost as bad as threats—playing on your niceness, Nan.'

'The price they offered is the best I'd get——' Nan said, not listening.

'But do you want to leave this house? Could you leave it Nan?'

Her grandmother's eyes flitted over the shabby, old kitchen with its ancient dresser fitted with a myriad of drawers and small doors and insets of leaded glass. She looked at the marble topped sink that was pitted but spotless as the day she had first used it as a bride. Her lips trembled and she put a veined hand to her eyes. 'Oh Fairlie, I don't know how I'd get along in some new place—one of those units or a rest home——'

Fairlie's eyes watered a bit as she looked through

the kitchen window, beyond the fence to the shattered remains of the Reynolds' house.

'Then you won't leave,' she said firmly and clasped Nan's hand. 'I won't let them drive you out.'

Her grandmother's hope was mixed with doubt. 'But the power cuts—I don't know if I can put up with that, and the washing—every day it comes in dirtier than it goes out and Fairlie, I'm ashamed to admit it, but I'm almost afraid to go out shopping. All those monstrous machines and the men drive near the gate like today. I don't suppose it's always on purpose, but——'

'You're too charitable, Nan. It isn't an accident that the only householder left around here is finding life difficult enough to think of leaving. And the awful thing is that shrewd Mr Tate has built such a wonderful, generous image for Colossus that even the press might find it hard to believe they would put pressure on a woman to leave her home. Or would they . . .?' She took out the keys to the earthmover and set them on the table thoughtfully. 'I think I might give these back to someone with a bit of muscle in the Colossus organisation. Tate himself if possible. But does he come up here to Brisbane very often?'

'He lives here—just temporarily I believe—but he's been away for a week and I don't know if he's back yet.'

'How do you know so much about him?'

'James told me.' She smiled. 'Now there's a nice young man. James—the same name as your grandfather. He won't answer to Jim either, just like my James . . .' She smiled again.

'Who is James, Nan?' Fairlie asked and Nan explained to her amazement and further dismay that nice young James actually worked for Colossus and dropped in to visit her from time to time.

'But if he works for *them*——'

Nan shook her head. 'No, James isn't up to anything nasty, I just know it. It's those legal people and a few of those men with the machines——'

Thank goodness she was here, Fairlie thought. Colossus was smart enough to send nice young James along to charm Nan, even while they made her life a misery. Eventually Nan would break down and admit that she just couldn't stand living with all the noise of the site and her dusty washing and nice young James, who so fortuitously shared the name of Nan's beloved dead husband, would comfort her and solve all her problems by getting her to sign a contract of sale. She should have come sooner, much sooner. Nan's letters had not betrayed the seriousness of her position. It wasn't until her aunt had returned from a visit here that Fairlie discovered her true plight. By then she was already planning to move in with Nan. Still, had she realised just how much Nan needed her, she could have cut a few corners. No wonder her grandmother was looking frightened. All her neighbours had gone. Some had been new—young trendies anxious to live near the city and full of restoration plans, but the Reynolds had been lifelong friends, links with memories of brides and young, struggling motherhood. Nan and Mrs Reynolds had swapped teething formulae, scone recipes, shared gallons of tea and sympathy through war and widowhood, death and disappointment. Nan's world, in spite of her independent loneliness since Pa died, had been the one she'd known since her marriage. Thanks to Colossus, all that was left of that world now was her home.

'I'm going to see Tate or your nice young James to

tell them that you're not going to sell whatever they do.'

'Dear, you will be—tactful, won't you? I don't want to antagonise anyone——'

Fairlie shrugged on her jacket, straightened the collar of her shirt and the tie, then pocketed the keys again.

'I've already antagonised them Nan. Sometimes attack is better than defence. But I'll be careful. I have no wish to turn up at my new job tomorrow with an earthmover's imprint on my legs.'

There was little movement on the construction site when Fairlie walked past it to the Colossus stage one building. Old Ripper was standing on the far side of the excavations, which seemed to indicate that they had abandoned their search for the 'keys' she had tossed them, and used the spares. She felt the turn of the workmen's heads as she marched along the dirt-caked footpath to Colossus' landscaped garden. A large sign advertised several 'prestige professional suites' available for lease in this building and numerous others soon to be offered at planning stage. The name of a nationally known property financier and an equally prestigious property agent featured on the sign along with Colossus. Nan must have created a few ripples on several large ponds, Fairlie thought. There was some wattle blooming in Colossus' garden. The scent of it tickled her nostrils and passed with her into the building foyer.

The directory board bore Tate's name in gold lettering. The tenth floor. Why have an office in Brisbane she wondered, remembering the very impressive Tate and Colossus office blocks in Melbourne. The tenth was quietly luxurious and

probably out of bounds to any but appointed visitors.
But she breezed through the gold knobbed glass doors
to the executive reception desk ready to wheedle her
way in to one of the top brass. The desk was empty.
Undecided, she looked at a memorandum on it
addressed to Ms S. Williams. Beside it lay a silver pen
engraved with the name SANDRA. That didn't help
much, she thought as she looked around and saw the
panelled door marked C. R. TATE. It opened and a
girl emerged, carrying some papers. Fairlie took a
gamble.

'Oh is Carson free then Sandra?' she enquired and,
taking advantage of the girl's surprise at the chummy
first names, went in and closed the door behind her.
Simple she thought, and smiled as she turned to look
around the office.

It was big. Huge. Sweeps of beige walls, gleaming
expanses of seamless glass. The carpet was a pale tan
sea and she was marooned on it. Fairlie swallowed
hard. Overpowering—but then that was typically
Tate. The large desk, a stunning antique in this
modern setting, was angled near a clear glass wall. A
similarly scaled chair stood empty and swivelled as if
the occupant had been gazing through the windows
when he left it. And why wouldn't he, Fairlie thought.
Clear glass looked out on to the outer wall of bronzed
glass. The city of Brisbane sprawled out—a permanent, growing mural for Mr Tate. From here he could
pick out all the bits he wanted to tear down.

Sandwiched between the walls was a terrace,
ceramic flagged and furnished with lacquered oriental
couches and tables. And everywhere there were plants.
Palms and bamboo and rampant monsteria. She
thought of those vague outlines of foliage glimpsed
from the ground. So that strip of tinted glass did mark

Tate's offices. If you could call this intimidating carpeted plaza an office. Where was the man himself though? There were other doors at the far end of the room. One was ajar. She felt for the keys in her pockets and suddenly felt like running away. The power of the man and the organisation was formidable. In this room she could almost smell it.

'Coward,' Fairlie muttered, oppressed by the surroundings. She comforted herself with the thought that most people would be wary of tangling with a Tate, even in Nan's extreme circumstances. There was the Tate Corporation for a start—everyone knew it and its rags to riches rise from the family construction business that grew into a multi-faceted organisation. The Takeover Tates. Ironically, their latest takeover was the construction giant Colossus. The papers had made much of the story. The battling family business financed forty-odd years ago by the Tate brothers' house mortgages—all grown up and swallowing Colossus which had been casting a giant shadow while the brothers were still trying to scrape up the funds for a pile driver. And now Colossus was being treated to the Tate magic—its plummetting profits lifted almost immediately by the son of one of the pioneering brothers. Carson Tate had also polished up the rather unattractive Colossus image with generous sponsorships to sport. Junior tennis championships, a major golf prize, the Colossus 1000 at Bathurst had turned Colossus into the gentle giant. The good guy. Ha!

As she walked near the glass wall, two doors slid open automatically. She stepped out on to the terrace. Far below, the iron roof of Nan's cottage was a pathetic geometric jumble of angles and peaks. From here none of the house's history of love and caring showed. It was simply a shabby old house. One that Colossus would not flatten if she could prevent it. Fairlie went back inside.

The door opened at the far end of the room and she caught a glimpse of books and easy chairs before the gap was filled by a man. He strode to the desk, eyes fixed on a sheet of paper in his hand.

'Mr Tate,' she said firmly and he gave a sort of absent grunt of acknowledgement without looking up. He sat down, continuing to read. She raised her voice.

'I've come to return something to you Mr Tate,' hoping she had the right man. Once she had seen Carson Tate on television, presenting some sportsman with one of Colossus' many trophies. It had been raining, she recalled and she'd gained no special impression of him beneath the black umbrella. Certainly not one of relative youth. He seemed only about forty. Younger even—late thirties. 'And to tell you that should you continue your harassments against Mrs Eliza Holborn, she will take legal action.'

His eyes flicked up from the paper. Just his eyes moved, nothing else. The attitude of barely arrested interest infuriated her.

'Mrs Holborn does *not* want to sell her property and I suggest, strongly suggest that you forget your mean, unscrupulous attempts to make her life so miserable that she will give in. Kindly inform your construction crew to park their vehicles on Colossus property, not across Mrs Holborn's gate as they did just an hour ago.'

'Why would they park across the gate?' he asked in a clipped, deep voice that had the grate of gravel in it. Fairlie's eyes flickered at this first sound from him. She didn't remember that voice from the rainy television appearance either.

'To prevent the owner from using it. And in this case to prevent me from getting in. I am now resident with Mrs Holborn.' She was pleased to see some reaction in those eyes at last. 'The defenceless, seventy-five year old widow alone may have been a target for your disgusting campaign. But I am a different matter altogether. You and your organisation don't frighten me.' What a laugh. She almost looked down to see if her knees were wobbling on the outside as well as inside. Driving the earthmover had been less unnerving than standing here!

Carson Tate's head came up. He leaned back in his chair. The paper was rested on the desk and his hands spread in ownership beside it. He had brows that dived together over a straight, dominant nose. He had an undistinguished mouth that was too thin by far on top and too full on the lower lip. There were lines deeply graven on the vertical at each side of his mouth and his hair—dark brown, almost black—was specked with silvery grey. It was a face that might have been drawn with a ruler. All straight, strong lines and angles. Not handsome but what a portrait subject he would make.

'You want me to have the machine shifted?' he enquired without much apparent interest, although she saw his eyes narrow on her in speculation. He would be difficult to paint. The eyes of the perpetual negotiator gave little away. There was strength there but few clues to the man behind the face.

'No. I did that myself,' she told him with some satisfaction. Carson Tate leaned a little further into his chair.

'Did you?' he murmured and she found herself under sharp scrutiny.

'I drove the earthmover back on to your site. If it is

left blocking our access again I will have it towed away. And I further suggest that you make some effort to lay the dust of your site before you begin work each day. There are legal steps I can take to ensure that Mrs Holborn is not inconvenienced by the dirt of your site. The site foreman will want these.' Fairlie slapped the keys down on his desk. The gesture made her feel good. In control. Almost. 'I think it would be wise Mr Tate if you had a talk with your construction manager and reverse his current instructions which seem to be to harass. If there are any more attempts to frighten Mrs Holborn into submission, you will face legal action and exposure in the press.'

He folded his arms. The sleeves of his shirt were rolled up. His arms were muscular, finely coated with dark hair that ran down as far as his wrists. A heavy gold watch was strapped about his left and on his right hand he wore a broad ring set with a diamond. It looked entirely masculine.

'Who are you?' he asked.

'My name is Fairlie Jones.'

Carson Tate gave her a complete once-over. If she thought she had already suffered his scrutiny this proved her wrong. Dark lashed grey eyes whipped up and down, lingered on the pulled back blonde hair and her mouth—skipped over the dark suit's severity. His mouth twisted as he looked at the shirt and tie.

'Ms?' he wanted to know. 'Or Mr?'

CHAPTER TWO

So he had a chauvinistic kind of humour, did he? Before she could resist the move, she raised her hand and checked the position of her tie. His eyes followed the gesture and she was unreasonably annoyed that she had made it.

'My sex is irrelevant, Mr Tate.'

He let his eyes drop lower to trace the feminine curves within the tailoring of her shirt and jacket.

'Oh, I wouldn't say *irrelevant*,' he murmured. 'Just not immediately obvious.'

Very funny, Fairlie thought, and steadfastly ignored this sidetracking. 'Mr Tate, I want some assurance from you that this harassment of Nan—Mrs Holborn will stop.' Irritably she noticed that his gaze had wandered to her hips and back to her breasts. 'Do you think you could possibly drag your attention away from my——' she stopped and felt a rush of heat to her face. What an idiot she was to let him goad her.

The grey eyes lifted to hers. 'From your——?' he prompted, well aware that she had driven herself into a corner.

'My figure,' she snapped.

'Ah. You disappoint me Ms Jones. I had a feeling you might have called a spade a spade.' His eyes slid over her once more, then he was cool, closed again. 'This Mrs Holborn whom you are representing—not your mother obviously—grandmother perhaps? You did say "Nan".'

'That's right. She moved into that house down there

23

when she was married. Her children grew up there—she wishes to stay there for her remaining years and I will do everything I can to ensure that she does just that. Your project will have to wait. Or you could of course simply buy more land and build your professional paradise somewhere else. I'm sure Colossus and the Tate Corporation have a dozen options.'

'And if I don't take all this advice you're giving me, Ms Jones, what then?' He leaned back again and fixed her with shrewd, assessing eyes. His lower position gave Fairlie no feeling of advantage—on the contrary, she felt vulnerable and exposed looking down at the man behind his huge desk.

'I'll take you to court if necessary, Mr Tate. I daresay that seems funny to you,' she added in a rush of anger at his half-smile. 'Like David taking on Goliath. But you might not like the publicity it would bring Colossus.'

'Colossus enjoys rather good press.'

'You've certainly paid enough for good press,' she retorted—'But your open-handedness might not look so good if it was known that your company was preying on one helpless person.'

There was a flinty look in his eyes. 'That could backfire on you Ms Jones. Your pushy manner wouldn't attract much sympathy even for a "helpless person".'

'Why Mr Tate, you underestimate me. Any publicity I arranged for our plight would naturally feature my grandmother, all grey haired and work-lined. And you might be surprised to see just how weak and defenceless I could look for a photographer.'

'Yes, I think I might,' he said drily. 'You're a

shrewd—er—*woman*——' He looked at her tie and hesitated deliberately over the description. 'But if you're holding out for more just say so. I haven't time for all this emotional appeal. How much do you want?'

Fairlie's deep breath tightened her collar about her neck. 'My grandmother has already been offered what she considers a generous price.'

'I imagine she has. But you would like to push that up a little? A natural enough wish I suppose for a close family member,' he said drily. 'How much, Ms Jones?'

It took her a moment to grasp his meaning and when she did Fairlie knew no amount of deep breathing would keep her temper on the leash this time.

'You—you despicable creature—do you think I'm only here to boost the price? Do you imagine I'm some sort of ghoul building on my grandmother's assets and waiting for her death?' Fairlie eyed the glass paperweight within reach on the desk and wished she could hurl it at him. Instead she whirled about and took a pace away from temptation. 'You think the situation can be solved by a bigger, better offer don't you, Mr Tate? Well, I have news for you. You could offer half a million and my grandmother would still rather live in the house that you no doubt think of as some shack standing in your way. But every uneven floor in that house, every papered shelf and rattling door knob means something to her. She has loved and grieved and nursed her husband and her children in that house and she loves it.' She paused, her chest rising and falling quickly with her angry breathing. Carson Tate watched her, apparently unmoved by her outburst. But he had drawn the paperweight towards him—to safety, perhaps? His fingers spread over its glassy surface. 'You can make your money anywhere,

Mr Tate—my grandmother has only *one* place that contains everything she holds dear. And I intend to make sure that she is not coerced or frightened out of it.'

'Coerced?' He picked up the word sharply. 'Spit the rest of it out Ms Jones.'

'Your tactics have been varied I must say. Oh, I'm aware that a man like you doesn't interest himself personally in that side of the business. You don't have to. You have staff who handle it all for you. I'm sure your underlings know what methods you approve.'

'Yes, they certainly do know,' he agreed with a certain grimness about his mouth. 'Your grandmother as far as I was aware, has simply been unable to make up her mind. What coercion has been used on her?'

'You think she's just a vacillating old woman don't you? She's not. But she *is* afraid and rightly so. She is severely and deliberately inconvenienced by the site work. Your people have been telling her that she is hindering progress, putting men out of jobs by delaying the work. Nan is rather susceptible to that line. She remembers the depression and your deputies have played on her guilt at denying wages to men with families. And,' her lip curled, '—one of your charming bright young men drops in to chat with her. I wonder if it is just a coincidence that his name is James—the same as my late grandfather. Those subtle tactics are rock bottom practised on an elderly woman stuck in the middle of your devastation.'

He flipped a switch on his intercom. 'Sandra, would you send Harvey in here, please?' To Fairlie he said, 'I've been away. This is all news to me. Sit down Ms Jones—take off your jacket, loosen your tie if you like.' It was what a man might say to another man and she fumed at the bland subtlety of the insult.

'No thank you. And whether you've been away or not, you have to take responsibility for Colossus' actions. What is this Mr Harvey going to prove?' she added impatiently.

The door opened before he could answer. A young man came in. A golden boy—fair hair, tanned skin, candid blue eyes and the kind of looks that hovered on the ordinary but which made a surprising impact. Seeing Fairlie, his eyebrows shot up. He made a brief but thorough inspection of her trim, tailored figure then smiled. Appealing dimples appeared and she almost found herself smiling back. Nice, she thought. This was the kind of man you couldn't help thinking was thoroughly nice. He worked for Tate so he had to be tough as nails surely, but what a superb façade.

'I'd like you to meet Ms Fairlie Jones. James Harvey, Ms Jones.'

She caught the mocking tilt of Carson Tate's mouth before she turned to the young man who came over to her, his thoroughly nice smile wreathing his thoroughly nice face. But he would admit to being anyone if the boss told him, she imagined.

'Your name really *is* James?' she said as he put his hand out to her.

'Well, yes——' he said, nonplussed and grinned. 'Ever since I can remember.' She put her hand into his warm grasp and was unable to prevent a smile in return. 'And is yours really "Jones"?'

'Ms Jones,' Carson Tate went on drily, watching the friendly little exchange, 'is Mrs Holborn's granddaughter. She has just moved in with her.'

'Really? How is Mrs Holborn? I dropped in to see her last week but haven't had time since then.'

'Quite frankly, Mr Harvey—the longer between your visits and anyone else's from Colossus, the better for my grandmother,' Fairlie said tartly and James sobered.

'Have you been upsetting Mrs Holborn—coercing her into selling her property to us, James?' Tate asked mockingly.

'I did mention it, naturally.'

'Naturally,' Fairlie echoed drily. 'And I suppose you hoped that all the little "inconveniences" she has been subjected to would make her decide to sell after all.'

'She did say she was having trouble with her washing and found the machines frightening,' James admitted in perplexity, 'I'm afraid I didn't think anything of it . . .' He sounded sincere enough. James didn't look as if he could tell a lie. She turned to Carson Tate.

'This doesn't seem to have achieved much except to establish that Mr Harvey didn't make up the name James.' The young man looked baffled and Tate waved a lazy hand and said: 'Ms Jones thought you might have introduced yourself as James because it was Mrs Holborn's late husband's name. To—er—ingratiate yourself.' He made it sound quite ridiculous.

'Good grief, I wouldn't do that,' James said, astonished and Fairlie had to believe him.

'Then I'm sorry,' she said.

'Ms Jones just moved one of the earthmovers, James,' Tate said. 'It was blocking her gate. Have a word with the crew and find out what's going on.'

James Harvey stared at Fairlie. 'You *drove* one of those things? You don't look strong enough.'

'Don't make that mistake,' his boss warned. 'I suspect that Ms Jones has nerves of steel under all her emotive oratory.'

Fairlie met his eyes steadily. Nerves of steel! She hoped he would go on thinking that.

'But to drive one of *those*——' James' amazement was tinged with admiration.

'I'm not Dresden china. I'll do it again if I have to—though I have to admit I'd prefer not to have to drive Old Ripper,' she added.

'Old Ripper?' Carson Tate raised his dark brows.

'The earthmover. She's a devil in reverse,' she said, absolutely deadpan.

Tate regarded her closely, as if he wasn't quite so sure about her. Hands in pockets, he came around to stand in front of her. He was taller than she'd supposed at first—but then his head had been bent over his papers. A big man, Carson Tate. Wide shoulders, deep chest. Strong, formidable. A rock. He took his hands from his pockets and set them on his hips. The stance made him more formidable than ever. The thoughtful look remained in his eyes.

'Leave it with me, Ms Jones. I'll look into your—claims, but I can't guarantee that I won't make your grandmother another offer. There's no immediate hurry but I want that land.'

'Well, Mr Tate,' she followed James to the door and looked back., 'even you can't always have what you want.'

'Miss Jones—Fairlie—I don't want to draw your fire,' James smiled at her as they walked to the lift, 'but you won't serve your cause by angering Carson like that.'

'Angering him! He looks too darned stony for anger—or for any other emotion either.'

James shook his head. 'You're wrong. Carson keeps it reined in pretty well but—could I give you some advice? If you see him again, act less—that is, act more . . .' He hesitated, his eyes dropping to her tie.

'Feminine?' she supplied. 'Flutter my lashes, wilt into a lacy handkerchief? Is that the kind of thing that brings out some compassion in your boss?'

He laughed. 'Good lord, no. Carson likes people to speak their mind but he can't abide aggressive women. You'd have more chance of getting your price if you——'

Fairlie turned on him, eyes flashing, just as the lift slid open with an electronic sigh. 'Price? Is that all you Colossus people can think about? I've told Carson Tate what I want, Mr Harvey, and it isn't money.' She stormed into the lift and left him standing with his thoroughly nice mouth open and a thoroughly nice hand stretched out.

'At least they know you're not alone any more,' Fairlie told her grandmother. 'I think that's about all my visit achieved. He really wants this land, Nan.'

'Oh dear . . .' Nan tutted but she seemed less concerned than she had been hours before. 'What is Mr Tate like?'

'He's a hard man. Tough. A bit younger than I thought though . . .' Fairlie looked through the window that was shut against the settling dust. The site was empty now of men. The machines were lined up like tame orange elephants. The site must be nearly ready for building to commence. It was perfectly understandable that they wanted this land. They were within their rights she supposed to expect it after Nan had made a verbal agreement. But their methods of 'persuasion' overruled any sympathy for Colossus' position. They had a fight on their hands now.

*   *   *

Nan's confidence returned at a rapid rate. She hummed along with a top forty number on the radio that was playing softly in the kitchen as it always had. Nan was of the radio generation. The greatest breakthrough of the technological age, she always maintained, had been the invention of transistors which had given her radio in the kitchen and released her from the big, old valve set that had dominated the lounge.

'Rock and roll, Nan?' Fairlie grinned.

'I like to keep up with the times,' she said. 'I like that Little River Band—but I love my classics. You run along, dear, and get your clothes sorted out. I'll make the dinner.' She shooed Fairlie out. 'Go on. You have your new job tomorrow and must get to bed early tonight.'

'Yes, Nan,' Fairlie said with a grin and left her grandmother happily chopping steak and kidney. Nan wanted someone to fuss over and for the moment her own bruised spirit wouldn't mind a little love and mothering. It was nearly four months since she'd given her ring back to Ben, bundled up his spare toothbrush and pyjamas and suggested he leave them at one of several other venues. Right to the end dear, charming, insincere Ben had been protesting that the other girl was just a passing fancy—a bachelor's final fling before settling into marriage. But though it had hurt she had looked into the future and known that for Ben there would always be passing fancies and she'd known too, that it would tear her apart trying to overlook them. 'I promise, Fairlie darling,' he'd said, just as he'd said once before. For Ben Ramsay promises were made to be broken. Fairlie sighed as she unpacked her suitcases. She really had had no luck with the men in her life. Her father—and Ben, both so fiercely loved. Both had let her down.

She heard the front doorbell, then Nan's voice in conversation. Minutes later she looked into Fairlie's room. 'It's that nice young James Harvey, he wants to speak to you,' she said and Fairlie looked with surprise at her pink cheeks and sprightly air. 'I've put him in the lounge—go and talk to him while I put the kettle on. There are a few of those scones left . . . you didn't say you'd met him dear——' She hurried away to the kitchen and Fairlie shook her head at the irony of it. So lonely was Nan, that even a call from a representative of the company that wanted her land was an occasion. Of course, James was a particularly pleasant representative as far as her grandmother was concerned. Fairlie wasn't at all sure that James was as nice as he seemed. Her mouth compressed as she entered the lounge, remembering his assumption that she was after a higher price.

He stood up, grinning awkwardly at her expression.

'I came to apologise,' he said at once. 'This business makes cynics of us I'm afraid and I assumed too much.' His smile was so charming, so earnest that she softened. 'Would you care to forgive me over dinner one night?'

'Dinner? I don't even know you,' she objected.

'Don't let that put you off—all I know about you is that you do stunts with the Colossus machinery, but I'm willing to go from there.'

She laughed. Her 'stunt' seemed to intrigue James. 'Hmm. I'll think about it. It hardly seems right to dine with the enemy.'

'I'm not your enemy. But if you think I might be, consider that it could be good strategy to dine with me.'

'Why?' she demanded. 'Would you tell me all Carson Tate's little weaknesses? What he plans to do to get us out of here?' Carson Tate's weaknesses. Was there such a thing?

'He won't do anything underhand.'

'Not *personally* he won't. Of course not. Mr Tate gets what he wants though doesn't he?'

He considered her carefully. 'As a rule.'

'This just might be the exception to the rule then, James,' she said lightly as her grandmother bustled into the room.

'You must be working late, James, if you're just on your way home from the office.' Nan puffed a little as she poured out tea. 'My, you must be the last one out again.'

'Not now that Carson is back from Melbourne. He works half the night sometimes—makes my efforts look puny by comparison.'

'And is he married, James?'

Fairlie rolled her eyes in exasperation. Carson Tate was determined to turn her out of her beloved home and here was Nan asking about his domestic arrangements. All the same, Fairlie couldn't suppress her own surge of curiosity about the man.

'He's divorced. His ex-wife married again recently.'

Smart girl, Fairlie thought. 'Don't tell me—*she* walked out on *him*. Am I right?'

James hesitated. 'So the story goes, but——'

Nan clucked, 'Divorced—oh dear. Were there any children?'

'He's got a son but he never talks about him much.'

'Such a shame for the children when there's a break-up like that . . .' Nan went on to reminisce over her own children's happy childhood and the lack of divorce in the family. James listened with every evidence of interest and Fairlie tried to imagine Carson Tate with a wife and son. It was easier to picture him as a loner as he was now, than as a family man. She almost laughed. Family man! With those cool, assessing eyes and that lack of any strong emotion. But there had been *something* ... She half listened to the ensuing conversation, unable to dismiss the Colossus chief from her mind. Something about those searching eyes clung to her with disturbing clarity.

James left with a renewal of his dinner invitation and Fairlie hedged, wondering at his persistence. He might be perfectly genuine, dining with him would be pleasant and unlikely to make any difference to the outcome of their battle with Colossus, but Ben had made her cautious.

'You should go,' Nan commented when he'd gone. 'He's a thoroughly nice young man.'

'But he works for the company that wants to move you out,' Fairlie cried, half amused, half exasperated. 'The same people who frighten you with their great machines that blow dust on your sheets.'

'Now James hasn't got anything to do with that,' Nan said firmly. 'And I daresay your Mr Tate mightn't either. Someone else would be in charge of all that.'

'He's not *my* Mr Tate, Nan.'

'No, well of course he's not, dear. Just a figure of speech. Fancy being divorced ... tsk, tsk ...' Nan busied herself with the dinner and Fairlie gave up. Nan had already decided upon her villains—the drivers of the machines and the legal men who'd been nowhere near as charming to her as James Harvey. And in spite of his power, Nan had decided sight unseen, that Carson Tate was somehow exonerated. It was just as well she was here to remind Nan that an enemy could wear the face of a friend. In fact she was the perfect person to do just that.

'Yes, you should go out with James,' Nan came full circle and Fairlie sighed. 'It's time you got back into circulation again.'

'What makes you think I haven't been back in circulation since Ben and I broke up, Nan?'

Her grandmother smiled indulgently at her and reached out to pat her hand. 'I can tell by looking at you dear. You can hide it from everyone else but not me. You're just like your mother, God rest her. She fought all her own battles on the inside too. If you ever feel like talking about it, Fairlie—or about your father . . .'

'Thanks, Nan,' she said shortly. 'But I'll be too busy with an exhibition and a new job to mope over what's past.'

Her job had been a stroke of luck. Sam Elliott, her former boss had come north from Melbourne two years ago to set up the Brisbane office of Rawlinson and Rawlinson, Insurance Brokers. When he left he told her to look him up in the unlikely circumstance that she ever wanted a job in Brisbane. She had 'phoned him from Melbourne and, as luck would have it, he was especially busy at present and his current secretary was leaving in six weeks. He agreed to hire her on a part time basis until Bronwyn left. Then Fairlie would take over her job. Financially it wasn't perfect—her bank account had never recovered from her six week tour of Europe—but the part time work would give her precious hours for painting.

'I am looking forward to seeing your exhibition dear,' Nan said.

Fairlie grinned. 'You might not care for it, Nan.

These aren't landscapes or portraits but a collection of abstracts. You've never seen any of my abstracts.'

Nan's face dropped. 'Do you mean those paintings of—um—nothing in particular?'

'That's one way of describing them I suppose,' Fairlie laughed.

'None of those lovely street scenes you used to do? No landscapes?' Nan asked hopefully.

'Not in this exhibition, Nan.'

'Well, I'm sure I'll like them anyway,' Nan said staunchly. 'More steak and kidney, dear?'

All in all, her arrival had done some good, Fairlie thought. At least Nan was much more herself—fussing a bit and wiping down her spotless kitchen counters with zest. Fairlie took the brown crock teapot out the back to empty it.

'On my parsley,' Nan directed and Fairlie found the small patch at the bottom of the back steps.

'Yoo-oo——' Nan called through the window after a few moments. 'You haven't got lost down there have you, dear?'

'Coming.' Fairlie's gaze was on the black bulk of the Colossus building. It was almost invisible against the dark sky fabric. A strip of light hung suspended there. High up. The silhouettes of palms were dark against the glass wall and for a moment Fairlie thought she could see someone standing there amongst the foliage—looking down.

The tea leaves sploshed on to the parsley. Fairlie ran up the steps and switched off the porch light hastily as if he might be watching. Stupid. It was too high and she couldn't possibly have seen Tate from down here. But he could see them—or the house at any rate. She knew that. The idea unsettled her. Even later as she nestled into her bed, she thought of the Colossus chief executive, alone in that building—looking down on them.

At six-thirty the next morning the site was growling with machinery. Dust billowed into the air and Fairlie rushed from her bed to close her window before the particles filtered inside. She stood a few moments, her body tight with frustration at the encroaching devastation held off, it seemed, only by Nan's ancient fence, and was about to turn away when she noticed the car. It had slowed down and the driver's head was turned towards the construction site. Impossible to see who was driving but the car was a grey Rolls which offered a clue. Fairlie peered through the lace curtains and saw the vehicle disappear into the underground car park of the Colossus building. Carson Tate. She threw on a gown and went to the kitchen with the tingling uneasiness of the night before. He would be in his office within minutes and able to watch them from his window. As she put the kettle on for coffee, she knew a grudging admiration for the man. He was top of the pile yet he made a six-thirty start after having worked late the previous night. It was obvious why he was divorced, she thought in sudden irritation at herself.

Nan bustled in, fully dressed, her silvery hair wisping about her face.

'Nan, do you still get up at the crack of dawn?'

'Around five-thirty,' her grandmother smiled. 'I like to get going early dear. Nowadays I water the garden before the men arrive next door.'

The kettle's steady hum wound down. 'Oh no, it's gone off again. Just when I'm ready for a cup of tea.'

Fairlie plugged it into another power point but the kettle didn't work. The power certainly seemed to be cut. But the kitchen light was still on. Fairlie frowned.

'The lights are okay but no power to the points . . . does this usually happen about the same time, Nan?'

'Sometimes it's late afternoon but mostly in the mornings. I don't know how many times I come in from the garden and find I can't boil the kettle.'

'*After* you come in——' Fairlie looked out thoughtfully at the workmen dotted around the site. 'Where's your fuse box, Nan?'

'Just under the back stairs—but now, you be careful . . .' she warned and followed Fairlie down the steps. Fairlie lifted the fuse box cover. The general power switch was on. The lights and hot water fuse were in place, but the power fuse had been removed and lay on the bottom ledge of the box.

'I think I've found your power problem, Nan,' she said and turned off the main switch while she gingerly clipped the fuse back in place. Hands on hips she looked at two of the men who cast a few glances over their shoulders as they walked away from Nan's fence. Her gaze lifted to the bronzed glass strip on their towering neighbour. 'Some people have none, while others have power to burn,' she muttered.

'What dear?' asked a bewildered Nan.

'I was talking about power. Come on, Nan, let's boil the kettle now that we've got some again.'

They made tea and coffee and Nan tut-tutted her distress when Fairlie explained what had been happening.

'Fancy coming over and turning it off—what a terrible thing to do. How can people be so nasty, Fairlie?'

'Maybe they're being paid to be nasty, Nan. I'll buy a catch and padlock after I've done my morning's work with Sam Elliott. But that will only solve one of our power problems.'

*   *   *

Sam Elliott greeted her enthusiastically at Rawlinson & Rawlinson's office, with reminiscences of her former efficiency, an offer of first refusal on a second-hand car and a pile of statistics he wanted her to work on over the next few weeks. It was a special report for head office, he explained, and too much to ask of Bronwyn, his pleasant and rather pregnant secretary who was, it seemed from her appearance, leaving a month too late.

'By the time you've compiled the report for me, Fairlie,' Sam Elliott beamed, 'Bronwyn will be ready to leave and you can take over her desk.'

Bronwyn looked as if she might not wait until the report was compiled and Fairlie made a mental note not to get stranded in the filing room or a lift with her—not without a Midwife's Handbook. She worked until midday then bought a sandwich and mooched around to reacquaint herself with the city. Then she bought a latch and padlock and caught a bus to Nan's place.

She was angry again at the sight of the house assailed by the dust and noise of the excavations. Even inside, the noise was loud and clear. Fairlie called Nan and as her voice died away, she realised that some of the noise *was* coming from inside. A chill feeling went with her as she followed the hammer blows to the back of the house. Nan emerged from the 'sleep-out', the closed in portion of the back verandah. Her cheeks were pink, her eyes the bright blue of excitement, her hair wisped with static. She was carrying a tray of empty cups.

'Fairlie, wait till I tell you! We have no need to worry at all—there's no question of me having to move and he's such a nice young man.'

James Harvey again, Fairlie thought suspiciously
and peered beyond Nan into the sleep-out which
appeared to be acquiring a new carpet. What was this
nice young man up to now?

'He stayed for tea and said he'd never had scones
like them—luckily I'd just made some for you and I to
have this afternoon——' Nan's brow puckered. 'I'm
afraid there aren't any left—you don't mind do you,
dear?'

Fairlie felt like screaming. There were men in the
house—Colossus men perhaps—and Nan was talking
about her provisioning. 'No, I don't give two hoots
about the scones, Nan. What are those men doing
here?'

'Oh, well now, he asked me if I'd rent them the back
room as a "site office" I think he called it—they'll pay
me for it of course, which will be a great help with my
pension and I'm going to cater for James' lunch and
teas—you know—and of course, they'll connect a
telephone which I can use if I want to after hours and
on weekends and not a thing to pay either. Now I
wonder if he'll be wanting a *hot* lunch every day, or a
salad—I must ask him . . .'

Fairlie followed the small, busy figure to the
kitchen. She was stunned. 'Do you mean you've
agreed to let Colossus use your house as an office?'

'Only the back room, dear—oh, and the bathroom,
of course. And naturally, I'd give James his lunch in
the kitchen if he'd prefer that, and if he wants a hot
lunch, well of course it would be better because . . .'

'Nan!'

'Yes, dear?'

'I take it James Harvey is going to occupy this
new—office?'

'That's right——' she flitted to the sink and

whisked up suds to wash the pile of cups and plates. 'I couldn't let the carpet layers go without a cuppa with their lunch,' she explained the dirty dishes happily to Fairlie.

After the carpet had been fitted, a carpenter would come to install the pine shelves that had already been delivered. And a gate was to be inserted in the side fence to give access from the main site. Thoroughly nice James had been very busy this morning. The enemy had broken through their front lines with a barrage of 'niceness' that had achieved more than all their scare tactics. Then Fairlie remembered.

'Nan—what did you mean he'd never had scones like them—James had some only yesterday.'

'Oh yes, *James* did—but not Mr Tate——'

Fairlie went cold. 'Carson Tate—he's been here arranging all this?' Tate—already dubbed a 'nice young man' by Nan?

'Yes, and he apologised for all the trouble. He had no idea it was going on. I told him you were going to put a padlock on the fuse box but he said to tell you not to bother. It won't happen again. He was *very* pleasant.'

'Was he really?' Fairlie said between closed teeth.

'I knew that was the way of it. An important man like that wouldn't know what was going on down here with the machines and such.'

'And did he make you another offer?'

'Yes he did, and handsome too. But when I explained that I couldn't think of living anywhere but here, he just said, "That's all right, Mrs Holborn, you've a perfect right to refuse my offer". That's when he asked about renting the back room. You're not upset about it are you, Fairlie?' Her grandmother eyed her anxiously. 'I mean, you can always use the verandah or under the house for your painting can't you?'

'That doesn't bother me, Nan. What does is that Tate is up to something.' Whatever it was, he was moving fast. Her head reeled at the speed of it. This morning when she left for work the sleep-out had been a store room—now it was almost an office. So much power to get things done.

'Oh I'm sure you're wrong, Fairlie, he's not a schemer. It was those legal men—tied me up in knots they did—and one or two of the workmen out there. He moved them you know—the ones who caused all the trouble. He wanted to sack them but I said no, I wouldn't like that even though they had been nasty. They were worried they might not get some special bonus or other if my refusing to sell held up the work. It was nothing to do with him. He couldn't be nicer. I can't understand why he'd be divorced . . .'

Fairlie closed her eyes. Twisted around Carson Tate's little finger—that was Nan. He'd played her exactly right—gained her confidence, convinced her that Colossus was a beneficent organisation, shunted the blame for her persecution on to a few anonymous parties and as his *pièce de résistance* had offered her the role of landlady and caterer—a role she couldn't resist after her long years of being unneeded.

'I'm going to see Mr Tate, Nan,' she said and her grandmother tut-tutted at her expression. 'Don't worry, I won't endanger your arrangements with him. I just want him to fill me in on a few details. Particularly the smell around here.'

Nan sniffed. 'Smell, dear?'

'The place is beginning to smell strongly of rat.'

CHAPTER THREE

SHE went to her bedroom and released her hair to brush it up again into a smooth, wisp-free knot. With shaking hands she smoothed the open collar of her blue silk blouse and brushed a few specks from her skirt. Fairlie had a helpless feeling suddenly. Power to burn, she had said this morning and it was all too true of Colossus. And Carson Tate. A fierce glow of defiance lit her eyes. She contemplated herself in the old-fashioned hinged mirror.

'There must be something you can do . . .' she muttered and reached for her perfume, spraying it liberally on her neck and wrists. The scent hung heavily in the air—expensive. Seductive. Fairlie snatched for a tissue to rub some of it off. Whatever sub-conscious suggestion had prompted *that* was erroneous. That was one method she wasn't willing to try on Carson Tate.

She could almost think she was expected. Sandra merely smiled as Fairlie went defiantly to Tate's door. The room was empty again. But now there was a sparkling new chrome framework supporting a model of the completed Colossus project. She studied it with a sinking heart. Offices, a shopping plaza, saunas and spas—but no room for Nan's house. Going by the plan, all traces of her home for fifty years would be smothered under a parking area and landscaping. People would literally drive all over her life. Whether or not Nan moved though, the project would go ahead. Strictly speaking, her land was not needed. The planned building took up almost a whole block with front entrances on a street parallel to Nan's and minor entrances on a side street. This building would retain its present access and Nan would have the back view of the complex—the parking lot and the supplier's route. It was worse in some ways that they could if they wished, go ahead without her land. But they weren't going to accept it anyway, were they? A battered old cottage perched amid all this brand new luxury.

She looked out on the terrace for Tate. There was a bar at one end she noticed this time—placed where the view over Brisbane was at its most spectacular, but there was no sign of the big man amongst the rioting plant life.

'In here, Ms Jones,' a deep voice bade her when she walked back near his desk and she glimpsed him through the door at the far end of the office. The half minute wait had robbed her of much of her impetus and she had to fight to throw off the feeling of oppression created by the office's proportions. But when she went to the sitting room, she was dismayed to discover that it was small. It was filled with bookshelves, several easy chairs and a tiny replica of the terrace bar on which stood an insulated jug and glasses. The scaled down proportions should have pleased her after the overpowering outer office, but instead she was aware of her escaping bravado faced with Carson Tate's dynamic shirt sleeved figure and the cosy afternoon tea setting for two.

He stood as she entered and the room seemed full of him. And of her recklessly applied perfume that was almost suffocating in the confined space. Perhaps he wouldn't notice.

'Won't you sit down, Ms Jones. Tea?'

'No thanks. I didn't come to socialise.'

He selected a biscuit from a plate.

'Really?' he mocked. 'Have something to eat then. I daresay there were no scones left for your afternoon tea. Your grandmother felt quite bad about it.'

It was said without the merest trace of sarcasm but Fairlie knew it was designed as a burr beneath the saddle. She burned with frustration.

'There are such things as mobile offices for construction sites—temporary buildings. You don't need an office in my grandmother's house.'

'But I do, Ms Jones. I need it very much.'

'Why?'

'Shall we say—liaison? After all the trouble your grandmother has had, I think it only fair that we keep an eye on our men and her welfare and what better way to do it than from her own house?'

'Garbage.'

'And she seems to rather like James,' he said softly.

'And you,' she accused.

'And me,' he agreed with modesty and lifted confident grey eyes to her. 'You might be surprised to see how very likeable I can be for sweet, old ladies.' Her paraphrased words sent her temperature sky high. How could she pierce this man with his overweening confidence. Arrogance.

Fairlie's mouth stiffened in contempt. 'You must want that land very badly, Mr Tate, to actually crawl out of the woodwork yourself and be *seen* to be pulling the strings. Oh, Nan might not be able to see what you're doing—you've read her very cleverly—brought a little excitement into her life, soothed her fears, given her the feeling of being needed that she's thirsted after since Pa died, and she thinks you're wonderful. And you know too that I wouldn't like to

take your little scheme away from her now that she's
so excited about it. But I *know* you're not the likeable,
kind, trustworthy man you've played for her—so
watch your step. You don't fool me for one moment
that you've set up a "site" office. We both know that it
is merely an excuse for proximity so that you can wear
Nan down to the decision you want. But while ever I
am around, Nan will continue to get both sides of the
story so don't count on bulldozing her house down
just yet, will you?'

'I never count on anything Ms Jones—particularly
where women are concerned.' He reached out and took
a stack of financial newspapers from the table and
actually leafed one open at a marker. The implication
was clear. He found what she had to say a bore. Fairlie
took the guard off her tongue.

'I'm glad you recognise your limitations. Your
success rate with females isn't one hundred per cent I
hear.'

That attracted his attention. Even elicited a flash of
anger but that was instantly repressed. He put aside
the paper and picked up the teapot, poured tea in the
second cup.

'I can only think you mean my divorce, Ms Jones.'

'Why—do you have *other* areas of failure with
women?'

He held out the cup to her, a mocking light in his
eyes. 'Not that I've noticed.'

Didn't anything faze him? Even a query against
his virility didn't pierce his superb self-confidence.
Fairlie squashed the feeling of distaste at her own
cheap effort to annoy him. If she had to war with
Carson Tate there was no sense in quibbling about
methods. But she resolved to steer clear of the
personal in future.

'That was a nasty blow,' he said. 'Below the belt so to speak. Take your tea. You look as if you need it.'

She took it and was immediately irritated that she had obeyed the compulsion of that outstretched hand. Sitting down with a bump, she set the cup on the table and some liquid slopped into the saucer.

'Careful, it's hot,' he warned.

'I *could* talk Nan out of this scheme of yours,' she said. 'You've made it difficult but if I wanted to I could dissuade her.'

He shook his head. 'Not on, I'm afraid. We have a contract—your grandmother and I.'

'What? You mean you actually got Nan to *sign* something?'

'I always get it in writing.'

'I'd like to see it.'

He shrugged. 'As you wish.' The single sheet of paper was conveniently located under the pile of newspapers. Afternoon tea for two? It struck her suddenly.

'Were you expecting me Mr Tate?'

'Of course, Ms Jones. I knew you'd want to come and give me a piece of your mind when you got home. And I have an excellent view.' He raised his teacup to his mouth for a moment, looking at her over it. Those grey eyes were less hard and cold today. It didn't please her much. 'You have a distinctive walk, even from up here.'

'You—watched me leave the house?' Fairlie was filled with the uneasiness she'd experienced last night, thinking of him up here, looking down.

'I saw you, quite by accident I assure you. I don't have time to stand watch.'

She took the contract and read it. Halfway through the simple, generous clauses she lifted her teacup and sipped from it, hoping to dispel the dryness from her mouth. The document seemed faultless. No wordy, ambiguous phrasing, no fine print. Any idea that this could be picked over by a solicitor was dashed. She took another mouthful of tea and swallowed the hot liquid hastily. This was an agreement designed to inculcate trust and Nan had signed it with probably the most cursory reading. How long would it take him to repeat the move—only with a contract of sale instead?

'Satisfied, Ms Jones?'

'No, I'm not. I won't be satisfied until you've re-designed your project around Nan's house or decided to use another site.'

'You know that your grandmother agreed initially to sell, don't you? If she'd made it clear from the start that she wouldn't move, we wouldn't have this problem.'

'And Colossus would have just run along and let her be? Ha! This building was started over two years ago. Colossus obviously has been planning to build the rest of the project around it since then. Why on earth didn't you acquire *all* the land before making your plans?'

'You're wrong. This building was underway when Tate's took over Colossus. It was a project lacking in foresight—a typical decision taken by the previous management. With the expansion in Brisbane and up north we were prompted to locate our own offices in it and to design a complex around it. Most of the land close by we already owned. Over some months we acquired the rest at more than generous prices as you can check for yourself. Mrs Holborn gave us no reason to believe that she wished to remain here.'

'What was that you said, Mr Tate? You always "get

it in writing"? Nan said that your representatives didn't ask her to sign anything for weeks after her verbal agreement. By that time she had changed her mind.'

'Yes,' his mouth was grim, 'that was sheer carelessness. And due to a few other errors our legal department wasn't even aware of the omission until we had made certain commitments. Had they performed properly your grandmother would by now be comfortably situated somewhere quieter and with considerable financial security.'

'You really believe that?' she scorned.

'Yes I do. After speaking with Mrs Holborn I can sympathise with her wishes to stay in an area she has known most of her life. Without her land our parking would be reduced and we would have to make changes in the design but even if we did that she will be faced with a great deal of change. She'll be in constant shadow, for one thing, there will be increases in the traffic, more noise, fumes and cars parked out front.'

It coincided with the picture she had drawn herself—deep down she knew that even if Nan managed to keep her house she wouldn't really have won. Everything around her would change yet again.

'How can you do this to her?' she burst out, all her hurt for Nan in her eyes.

'Take a look at the district. It's almost part of the city now. If it wasn't Colossus it would be someone else—you must know that Fairlie,' he said softly.

Her hand jerked. The tea spilled and she gasped as it showered the front of her blouse. Carson Tate leapt from his chair and took the cup from her fingers, preventing her from spilling the rest on herself. He snatched the bar towel up and began sponging the wet stain, lifting the fabric away from her skin.

'Leave me alone.' She twisted as his hand dabbed at her chest. 'It's not that bad.' It was stinging, throbbing, but his touch was worse.

'Don't be a fool,' he snapped and flipped open the insulated jug to pour ice water on to the towel. 'Hold this,' he commanded and folded her hand so that she held the towel against her chest. Her eyes were watering from the pain of the burn and she obeyed. But she exclaimed as he tugged her blouse from her waistband and slipped the buttons.

'What are you doing?' she grabbed at his wrists, but her blouse was hanging wetly open and he merely took the towel from her flailing hand and pressed it to the red, blotched skin over her breasts. The ice cold pressure felt good, good enough to make her still and look up at the man. He raised his eyes from her chest and held her gaze.

'This will stop your skin from blistering,' he said quietly.

It was the closest she'd been to him and now, with her eyes watering and her skin stinging, was hardly the moment to notice things she hadn't before—that he had more lines on his face than she'd supposed. They weren't unattractive. Just signs that he had at some time been at the mercy of emotion. He had laughed, she thought, seeing the rays of lines at his eyes and maybe he'd even cried a little at some time. Not recently though. Carson Tate was not a man of emotion now. There was nothing she could read of the present in this imperfect face. Nose too dominant, she decided—and his mouth was all wrong. Had some of his lower lip fullness been given to the upper it would have been a handsome mouth. But there was a strength of line to his face. She let her eyes wander along the powerful shape of his jaw, to the jutting chin then along the lower, sensual lip and strong vertical of his nose ... all this she saw in seconds. Her face warmed as she met those eyes again. He smiled faintly at her interest and removed the towel to pour more ice water on it. Fairlie looked down at herself, suddenly aware of just how exposed she was. Her bra was sheer lace and low cut. With another exclamation she raised her hands to fasten her blouse.

'Not yet,' he said and pushed her arms away. In a sort of fascination she watched his large hand press the towel to a red patch low on her breast where the lace just covered her nipple. His ring gleamed gold, the diamond flashed as he moved a little. Once again she was still, startled by her reaction to the sight of his hand on her. And the feel of it. As he shifted the towel, the warmth of his palm closed over the underswell of her breast. Fairlie drew back sharply. She looked into grey eyes that were warm and close. Too close. There was a spark of something new in them. He looked down at the burn.

'Shall I kiss it better?' he murmured and actually lowered his head. Fairlie jerked away, seeing too late the wicked, satisfied curve to his mouth. Carson Tate—teasing? And rather sexy at that. Her fingers shook and she muttered as she tried to button the damp blouse.

'Here,' he put hands to her shoulders and spun her around.

'I can do it,' she insisted, fighting against him.

'Don't be silly,' Carson Tate chided and impersonally fastened three lower buttons while she struggled with the first. As she tucked the blouse into her skirt he stood looking down at her. Quite a long way down considering her own above average height.

'If you expect me to say thank you, you can forget

it,' she told him, trying to regain the initiative. 'All that was quite unnecessary.'

'You might thank me eventually. It wouldn't be too comfortable to have blistering burns on your . . .' his eyes dropped to her cleavage, 'figure.' He grinned as her chest heaved in renewed anger. His face was radically altered by the full smile. It drove the lines deeper beside his mouth but banished the frown that habitually drew his brows into a vee. He had strong, white teeth that were a trifle uneven. It made his smile more boyish than perfectly straight teeth might have done. She was seeing what Nan had obviously seen— though Fairlie wouldn't go so far as to describe him, even looking like this, as a 'nice young man'.

She went to the door. 'What I said stands. I don't know what you're planning but be careful. I smell a rat.'

'You amaze me.'

'Why? That I don't know what you're planning? My mind isn't so devious.'

'No. That you can smell a rat.' He sniffed. 'Almost impossible to smell anything but . . . is it *Chanel*? French anyway. You must have used a few dollars' worth before you came to see me. Really, Fairlie, you shouldn't have.'

'I spilled the bottle,' she lied.

'Two spills in one day. Not nervous about coming to bawl me out were you, Fairlie?'

'I'd be an idiot if I wasn't nervous.'

He seemed surprised at the admission. 'Of me in particular or of Colossus?'

'You, Colossus—that——' she pointed to the project scale model, 'all make me very nervous, Mr Tate.'

'It wasn't that kind of anxiety that made you scald yourself,' he observed. 'Why did you? I said nothing to upset you. In fact I was being very pleasant I thought.'

'That was it I expect,' she said drily. It was because he had sounded sympathetic, understanding all at once. And he had used her name—said it softly in that deep, rough-edged voice.

'I was pleasant and you were surprised enough to scald yourself?'

'You weren't exactly Prince Charming yesterday.'

'Neither were you, though you looked the part.' He half smiled and watched her tighten up at his reminder of the mannish clothes that had given him so much occasion for sarcasm. 'You know you really didn't have to go such—pains—to convince me that that shirt and tie hid a woman.'

She flushed. 'Don't be ridiculous. I couldn't care less about your sexist comments yesterday. They were typical of the threatened male.'

'Threatened?' he sounded amused and came to lean in the doorway.

Fairlie stepped back and he grinned. 'Threatened Fairlie?' he said again. 'By your shirt and tie?'

'It does seem to bother some men.'

'I'm not some men.'

For once she agreed with him. He certainly wasn't like any man she'd met. Turning away, she walked the carpeted plaza to his office door, conscious that he was behind her. She tried not to let her leavetaking look like a retreat. When she looked around he was at his desk.

'Remember what I said Mr Tate. I'll be watching you.'

'I'm flattered.'

On an exclamation of annoyance she wrenched the door open. 'I'll be back if I discover the slightest thing out of place. And I'll bring legal assistance next time.'

'That could be expensive,' he said. 'Next time try Givenchy instead.'

She slammed the door and paused outside it to collect her composure. Sandra stared at her tea-stained, crumpled blouse and so did the other occupants in the lift. Fortunately Nan was in the kitchen when she got back and Fairlie was able to remove the garment before she saw it.

The skin on her chest was red and painful. Fairlie leaned toward the mirror to trace the splotches with one finger and recalled with crystal clarity the sight of Tate's hand moving over her skin. 'Shall I kiss it better?' . . . she hurled the wet blouse on to her bed.

Fairlie completed her second half day of work on Sam Elliott's statistical report. She said goodbye to Bronwyn who was wearing several metres of flowered smock, and walked to the Van Lewin Gallery to be overcome—again—by Pieter Van Lewin's mammoth charm.

Pieter was fifty, fabulously fair and built on an operatic scale. When she entered he taxied—arms outflung—hands outspread—down the entire length of the gallery. 'Fairlie—my sweet Fairlie——' he bellowed in a voice that shook the chains supporting his current exhibits, and she tensed as she always did, lest he forget his size and strength and crush her. But Pieter took her shoulders as ever with exquisite care—as if she was a piece of porcelain—and kissed her on both cheeks.

'Pieter, it's so good to see you again,' she smiled. 'Even if I have to adjust my vision to Cinemascope.'

Pieter Van Lewin, once within arm's length, filled

every bit of peripheral vision. He literally walled the background from view and dressed as he was now in one of his pastel shirts, he resembled a lumpy double bed made up with floral sheets and turned on end.

'Ah,' he sighed and his stomach trembled. 'You know the saying darling—the bigger they are, the harder they fall.' He took her hand and kissed it with a courtly air, sighed again. 'If I was only twenty years younger——' He looked at her with soulful blue eyes. 'And five stone lighter.' His laugh rumbled from his mighty chest and Fairlie laughed with him in this standard scene she'd played with Pieter on and off for two years.

He inspected her hand more closely, and eyes suddenly shrewd flicked to hers. 'What happened to that delightful diamond ring you were wearing last time I saw you?'

Fairlie looked away. 'Oh, that's old news, Pieter. Ben and I broke up nearly four months ago. In May.' The merry month of May.

He pursed his mouth in sympathy. 'I haven't been home to Melbourne since April so I hadn't heard. I assumed he was moving up here with you.' He paused. 'My dear—I won't say "I told you so".'

'No,' she said lightly, 'please don't will you? Ben would never have been able to settle down to marriage and I—well—we parted friends.' Even after his betrayals she couldn't truly hate Ben. She might never see him again, but she would never hate him.

Pieter shook his head, dislodging a few of the carefully distributed blond strands that inadequately covered his scalp.

'Lovers, then friends—I wonder if that's possible,' he murmured and put up a massive palm to scoop his hair back back into place. 'But, my darling Fairlie—

you have your art—and more to the point, I have your paintings. They arrived this morning. I think I can sell some for you. Three, four perhaps, no more than that in today's climate, but enough to grease the wheels, eh?' He slid an arm about her and walked her down the gallery, giving her details of the work displayed interspersed with his arrangements for her own exhibition. 'And,' he finished up, 'I have an old friend from Sydney coming to see me while your paintings are on show. There's a chance—just a chance you mark, that I might be able to talk him into taking your work. He has a joint showing coming up and one of his exhibitors has suddenly had an attack of temperament. You could well be just what he needs.'

'Pieter, that's marvellous. You're too good to me. I'm so grateful.'

The big man sighed. 'Grateful—ah, you know how to wound me Fairlie darling. If things had been different, it wouldn't be gratitude you'd be giving me.'

This was a scene they'd played too, many times. Fairlie grinned. 'You mean your advanced age, Pieter?'

Gloomily he nodded. 'Double yours. Unkind fates to let me be born so soon. And what beautiful, talented girl would marry a man twice her age and twice her weight?'

'You could always try dieting, Pieter.'

'Dieting? Fairlie my fairest, would you take from me my one consolation? If I can't have you, at least I can have my seafood and my sauces——'

'And your crêpes and your strawberries Romanoff—and your brandied peaches and your roast pork and . . .'

'Stop, stop,' he groaned. 'I haven't had lunch—you

are killing me. Come, console me with coffee and confidences.'

And what a relief it was to tell it all to someone. Pieter watched her carefully as she related Nan's problems and her own two confrontations with Carson Tate and the negative outcome. And although she scrupulously avoided anything personal he seemed to know that she was more disturbed than she liked by the Colossus boss.

'He is a formidable man in business I hear—like his family,' Pieter commented. 'And not so bad in private either.' He noticed her quick curiosity. 'He is currently seen with Geraldine Hallam—a customer of mine from time to time, and a very choosy lady.'

'Have you met him Pieter?'

'No, I have not. But—I think, I would like to. You find him attractive?'

'How could I find a rat like him attractive Pieter?'

He smiled at her and she thought for a moment that his blue eyes looked pensive even though his cheeks contracted and the laugh lines near his temples deepened.

'Strange things happen between men and women, Fairlie darling. Here am I a mountain of a man—too old and all wrong for you, but *mad* about you. And you, beautiful and warm, mad for worthless Ben Ramsay . . . life is a big joke is it not, Fairlie?'

She laughed uneasily, warned by the slight foreign intonation that Pieter was cloaking seriousness beneath his amusing manner. But which part of his statement had resulted in that stiffened English? She began to defend Ben, but changed her mind. Pieter had always maintained that Ben was not good enough for her and she had argued it with him on several occasions at his Melbourne gallery where she had met him. But she had to admit, some of what he had said had turned out to be true.

'Call anytime, my dear,' Pieter told her when she was leaving and pressed a card into her hand. 'Ring me at home—my number is on the card. I've found a charming house in Rainworth. So charming in fact that I'm negotiating to buy it from the landlord. Then I can fly up here every time the Melbourne weather turns nasty.'

'You're thinking of spending most of the year here then,' she grinned.

'Just so my sweet. If you want to seek legal help for your grandmother let me know and I'll introduce you to my own solicitor here.'

'Thank you, Pieter. I'm very——' she was about to say 'grateful' again when she surprised a flash of something like anger in his blue eyes. It unnerved her—Pieter had never, in all the time she'd known him, been angry with her, '—glad to be here. Will you come to dinner one evening? My grandmother won't cook any of your elaborate gourmet dishes but she does a wonderful traditional roast dinner with gravy, baked vegetables and steamed pudding and custard to follow—maybe a little whipped cream or brandy butter——' she added provocatively.

Pieter groaned, 'Yes, yes, yes! Go now—quickly, you temptress.' Fairlie stood on her toes and kissed his cheek. 'It's so good to see you again Pieter.' And she went without turning back, wondering why the big man's predictable effusion had struck her as somehow different this time.

As she alighted from the bus at Nan's house, she decided it was *her*. She was so uptight about Colossus and Nan's danger of being taken over. And about him.

Carson Tate. Involuntarily she looked up at the tenth floor before she opened the gate, then quickly down again in case the man should be watching. She didn't want to give him the impression that he was on her mind. But he was. And when she went inside to discover that the sleep-out had been completely transformed during the day and fitted out with desk, shelves, filing cabinet and a 'phone—the last of which took any ordinary person weeks or months to obtain—her heart sank. Nan's days here were not only numbered, they were numbered in single figures by the look of it. But her own presence here must be a thorn in Mr Tate's side, Fairlie thought with satisfaction. A granddaughter with her wits about her and a fair share of cynicism was not going to make his task easy. How, she wondered was Mr Tate going to deal with her?

It took her more than a week to find out. During that time James Harvey moved into the 'office' apparently rather baffled by it but cheerfully willing to do Tate's bidding. Nan, already fond of him, took him to her heart.

'You're just like Leila's boy—isn't he, Fairlie?' she said once. 'Cecil. Always so polite and good looking too.'

James always listened to Nan as if he was truly interested and Fairlie wondered if she was being unduly suspicious to doubt it. He brought a Little River Band tape with him once when he found out that Nan liked the group and she played it for hours while she crocheted in the lounge room. Fairlie dodged a definite answer each time James reiterated his invitation to dinner but it was with steadily declining resolution. He came across her on the verandah late one day, hammering together stretchers for her canvases.

'Your grandmother told me you paint. What kind of things apart from "modern ones about nothing in particular"?' His face dissolved into his dazzling smile and Fairlie laughed.

'Nan won't like my abstracts. I know it and she knows it but she'll try her darndest to find something in them out of sheer loyalty.'

His questions revealed his ignorance of the subject but also an endearingly open mind to something he admitted frankly was baffling. His bluer than blue eyes were earnest, admiring and Fairlie felt a flicker of pleasure—one of the few she'd experienced with a man since Ben. He pressed her again to go out with him.

'I know a place that serves French food and exhibits contemporary paintings on its walls. You could explain them to me. And the menu too. It's in French.'

'What makes you think I could read the menu?'

'Your grandmother told me you speak French.'

'Well—it's very rudimentary French as I found out when I went to France.' She frowned. Just how much did Nan tell over those teacups and scones and hot lunches? And what did James relay to his boss? She belted more timber pieces with the hammer.

When she paused James said, 'It's all right Fairlie— I don't tell him anything about you.'

'Him?' she repeated carelessly.

'Carson.'

'Oh. Why should that bother me anyway?' Good question.

'But it does, I can tell. Fairlie I don't know what happened last time you saw him, but——'

She stood up, hoping the news of her tea-stained blouse hadn't reached him. 'Yes James.'

He blinked. 'Yes?'

'I'd love to have dinner with you.'

Her restlessness increased even though life had slipped into an apparently easy rhythm. If you could ignore the new hoardings around the site and the roar of the machines outside Nan's fence. And Nan, it appeared, could. The men were taking care to lay the dust around her back garden by the use of hoses and they started work with the machines later than previously.

'Mr Tate arranged it,' she told Fairlie one evening. 'Isn't that considerate of him?'

'Is it? Nan, you know that even if he gives up and builds around you there'll be a shadow over the house nearly all day, don't you?'

'Yes dear and I hate the thought of it, but there—I hate the thought of leaving my dear old house more, as I told James and Mr Tate again this morning.'

'He was here again? Tate?'

'He just dropped by—such a gentleman. So anxious to do the right thing. You must try to see the good side of him Fairlie.'

'What did he talk about?'

'Me mostly. I'm afraid I ran on a bit, but it's so nice to be able to chat about the old days. He's an only child too, like you.' She sighed. 'He's a lonely boy I think and I'm glad we got to know him. You wouldn't credit it would you—that something so upsetting could turn out so well?'

Lonely boy? Carson Tate? Fairlie refrained from the comment that sprang sourly to her lips and instead answered, 'I'm not so sure it has turned out well. I have a feeling that you're more in danger of takeover by niceness than you ever were from open skullduggery.'

But Nan refused to believe it and Fairlie went to work each day with misgivings, wondering if her grandmother might be sweet-talked into signing away the house that she dearly wanted to keep.

The statistical report for Sam Elliott took shape as she whittled down the pile of records. As the documents diminished, Bronwyn's figure increased and her serenity seemed to Fairlie to be a sign of unawareness. Bronwyn had about her the air of someone who could well be surprised at the onset of labour—someone who could have seriously miscalculated and Fairlie nearly jumped out of her skin one day when the woman screwed up her face in pain.

'Oh no—Bronwyn—Mr Elliott——' Sam Elliott was out and she went reluctantly to Bronwyn and patted her shoulder. 'Everything will be all right—we'll just stay calm and 'phone your doctor——'

Bronwyn giggled. 'No need for that,' she said cheerfully, 'I can look after it myself.'

'What?' Fairlie leapt away from her.

'It's just a scratch.' She craned her neck to see her shin. 'I knocked my leg on the desk.'

'Oh——' Fairlie muttered something in embarrassment—and relief. Bronwyn thought it a huge joke.

'It's lovely of Mr Elliott to keep me on so long. We really need the money. But I'm not due for another six weeks you know.'

Fairlie nodded and went back to work. 'So you say,' she murmured.

Sam Elliott seemed horrified when Fairlie shared her anxiety about Bronwyn with him.

'You don't think she could suddenly——' He peered

out at his tranquil secretary. 'No. That sort of thing doesn't happen nowadays Fairlie. Besides she's leaving in a month and the baby is due weeks after that.' But Fairlie couldn't help thinking that if Bronwyn bumped her leg again and Sam Elliott saw the resulting grimace, he would have an ambulance dispatched within minutes.

The second-hand car that Sam had mentioned on her first day turned out to be a sedan, the property of a friend of a friend whose various interests were represented by a barrage of stickers over the windscreen and bumper. Some souvenir stickers bearing place names seemed to indicate that the car had been around the entire Australian continent on Highway One. The mileage confirmed it and Fairlie knew she was taking a risk. But she inspected it in the office car park, took it for a drive during which it performed well enough and she decided that for the price, it would do. At least, she told Sam, she would have some means of conveying Bronwyn to hospital in an emergency.

She drove home, pleased to have some transport again and thinking of drives out to Moreton Bay or to the mountains with Nan. But as she let herself into the house, the sound of a male voice in the lounge put an end to her pleasure. As she went to the door, Nan was saying doubtfully: 'I don't know if I should do that Mr Tate——'

Fairlie judged it time to enter. As the door opened Carson Tate said, 'I'd very much like it if you would, Mrs Holborn.' His eyes went to Fairlie as he finished speaking and he stood up immediately, holding her gaze all the time.

'*What* would you very much like, Mr Tate?' she demanded, not even glancing at Nan who was fluttering about putting milk in the spare cup on the tea tray.

'So suspicious, Fairlie,' he chided.

'With good reason. What charming demands are you making of my grandmother now? And have I arrived in time to prevent you getting it in writing?'

'In writing?' He was openly amused now and Fairlie darted a look at Nan who was tutting a bit at her plain speaking.

'Fairlie dear, do sit down. Mr Tate wants me to call him Carson and normally I wouldn't have the slightest hesitation but we have a business arrangement and it doesn't seem businesslike to use first names. And he is an important man——' She waved away Carson's modest disclaimer at that.

'Perhaps *Sir* Carson would be appropriate,' Fairlie said tartly and Nan's eyes flew apologetically to Tate.

'That might be a little premature,' he said in utter blandness.

'Oh.' Nan's eyes were round. 'Do you think one day you might be——?'

He laughed, a low, deep chuckle and shook his head. 'No, I doubt it Mrs Holborn.'

'Have you found something money can't buy Mr Tate?' Fairlie enquired. Carson's smile faded. He ran cool grey eyes over her.

'There are always things money can't buy, Fairlie.'

CHAPTER FOUR

'Sit down and have some tea dear,' Nan offered her a cup and Fairlie subsided into an armchair with it.

'Careful,' Tate murmured, eyes on her open neckline. 'You don't want to burn yourself.'

To her dismay, her cheeks flamed. Damn him, recalling that stupid scene. She bent her head over her cup but not before he had noticed her colour. As her grandmother went on talking Fairlie felt those eyes touch her from time to time.

Rising she put her empty cup on the tray. 'I have things to do Nan, and I'm sure Mr Tate is eager to get back to work.'

'Not eager, but I must go. You stay there and finish your tea Mrs Holborn. Your granddaughter will see me out.'

Fairlie was edged out into the hall by Tate's advancing figure. 'You're very experienced at manipulation Mr Tate,' she said in a low voice, her teeth clenched. 'On a small scale as well as large. I take it you wanted to say something to me.'

She stopped near the front door and he took her arm and swept her further on to the verandah which trembled from the vibration of the Colossus machines.

'Just a piece of advice Fairlie.' He had not let her go and she was close enough to feel the warmth he exuded—to be aware of the sheer masculine power that relied she realised now, not on large impressive offices or the trappings of wealth, but on something intrinsic in the man. And far more daunting.

'Advice, Mr Tate? This sounds uncommonly like a veiled threat coming up. Are you going to advise me to join you in persuading Nan to sell to you?'

His hand tightened on her arm. 'I need this land—I make no secret of it. But I believe there must be some way for both your grandmother and me to have what we want.'

'No way. What possible compromise could be drawn between one who wants to hold on to a few simple things and one who wants to make another million or two?' Incredibly she saw that she had pierced his armour. There was more than irritation in the set of his mouth and those steely eyes. 'But please, let me hear this advice you feel you must give me.'

'I'm aware that the situation has been mismanaged from the start. Our financial partners are on my back over the affair and we need a solution. While we work this out it would be a help if you abandoned your hostile attitude, Fairlie. It serves no useful purpose and it upsets your grandmother.'

Her mouth opened and shut, opened and shut in astonishment. The sheer gall of it!

'You hypocrite! It's not me that had Nan reduced to a grey little old lady who was frightened to go out to do her shopping. It's not *me* who threatens to enclose her home with great, soulless buildings or relegate her to a flat or a retirement home. What would *you* know about what upsets her—and what do you care? In spite of your smiles and cosy chats, you haven't got a warm current in your body. All this sudden charm is so much hype to get what you want. But money is your metier Mr Tate—not people. You're wasting your time trying to weasel your way into people's affections. You're bound to be found out——'

His irritation burst into anger. It was a triumph to

have evoked at last, some strong reaction from Carson Tate. Even when he gripped both her arms and glared down at her, she was pleased as much as afraid. And curious too. Why would such a petty insult weigh with him? She'd said worse to him before, much worse and seen nothing more than faint amusement in those grey eyes.

'What's the matter Mr Tate—I thought you *liked* plain speaking.'

James emerged from the house, stopping in the doorway as he saw them. 'Sorry if I'm—interrupting,' he began and eyed Carson's hands on her with speculation.

'It's all right James.' Carson let her go. 'Did you want me?'

'No. I'm coming up to the office in a minute but I wanted a word with Fairlie first.'

'Go ahead. I'll wait and walk up with you.' Tate said and folded his arms with a look of immovability though he must have guessed James wanted a few minutes of privacy.

'Oh. Okay.' James smiled at Fairlie. 'Seven-thirty tonight?'

She made her smile brilliant, sympathising with the younger man's rather embarrassed air.

'Lovely James,' she said in her huskiest tones. 'Shall I put in my phrase book? My French is a little rusty.'

James grinned, shafted a sheepish glance at his boss who was making no attempt to hide his interest.

'Even rusty French would be an improvement on mine.'

'Is there a band?' she enquired, doggedly determined to pursue the conversation in spite of Carson's presence. Or rather, because of it.

'Yes, quite a good one.'

'Going to let your hair down Fairlie?' Tate asked,

eyes mockingly on her sleek, drawn back hair. 'Putting on a new shirt and tie for the occasion?' His eyes roved her tailored work clothes.

'I don't know,. She gave it some consideration. 'Will they let me in without a tie James?'

James laughed. 'Take that, Carson.'

His boss merely smiled. 'Are we finished James, or do you need additional time for your wooing? I believe you do have another engagement?' The sarcastic tone brought a flush to James' face and Fairlie's sympathy grew. What an insensitive boor Tate was.

'Seven-thirty then.' James took her hand and she pressed it warmly.

'Is that your car, Fairlie?' Carson asked as he passed her.

'Yes.' She looked over at the sedan parked in the footpath driveway. It looked rather gaudy with its blue and white colour scheme and stickers patched on it. She had one problem with the car. Although there was ample room for it in Pa's old car garage under the house she couldn't use it because the vehicle gate, unmoved since his death, was jammed.

'Better not leave it there—you're contravening council ordinance—er—twenty-four. Or so I believe,' Tate murmured and Fairlie stared at him. He really *had* investigated her complaints personally if he knew about that rather ridiculous threat of hers.

'The gate bolt has rusted into the concrete, so I'll be parking in the street,' she said shortly.

She took out her feelings on a canvas, relishing the release. It was pure indulgence and artistically of no value whatsoever. But the aggressive painting did wonders for her morale. Nan found her on the verandah in the failing afternoon light by which time

Fairlie had almost rid herself of Tate-hate. The resulting canvas was heavy with paint—charcoal and lighter greys and a turmoil touched with vermilion.

'What do you think, Nan?' she asked and grinned at her grandmother's hastily masked feelings.

'I don't know that I understand it,' she put her head on one side as if a different angle might give her a clue, 'but it looks very angry.'

'Got it first time Nan. I think I'll it "Sir Carson".'

Nan clucked her distress. 'Couldn't you try to like him a little, dear—he's making such an effort to be pleasant.'

'He doesn't know the true meaning of the word, Nan.' She surveyed the painting through narrowed, critical eyes. 'If Pieter saw this he'd probably change his mind about exhibiting my work.'

'You must bring Mr Van Lewin home for dinner Fairlie—what is he like?'

'Pieter's cultured, charming company and a very shrewd man. He's Dutch.'

'Married?' Nan asked.

'Once a long time ago. It didn't work out.'

'Oh dear. So he's single. And wealthy I suppose with galleries all about the place?'

'Only two—Melbourne and here in Brisbane. But he's comfortably off.' Fairlie smiled at Nan's probing. 'I've already mentioned dinner here and he's keen to come.'

'That's lovely—I can do a nice roast. I hope he's a man who likes his food.'

Fairlie managed to check the quiver in her voice. 'Yes Nan, I think you could say he likes his food. And he is very charming. You'll like him.'

'Well—he sounds just like Mr Tate.'

'No—he's *twice* the man that Mr Tate is.'

*　　*　　*

She tried to tell herself that it wasn't Tate's sardonic remarks that made her wear her hair loose for her date with James. And she tried to tell herself that she didn't wish the big man of Colossus could see her dressed like this instead of in her working clothes. In a strapless eau-de-nil dress of crêpe with her streaky blonde hair loose and waving about her face she bore only a small resemblance to the neatly groomed image she kept for the office.

'So much like your mother——' Nan beamed. 'Except that you've got your father's chin I could swear I was looking at Felicity. Lovely, dear.' She paused. 'Have you heard from your Dad lately?'

'Two months ago. It was postmarked Calgary, Canada.'

'I wonder what he's doing up there . . . poor man.'

'Yes,' Fairlie said tightly. 'Poor man. That must be James.'

'I won't need any help with my French superlatives,' James said as he took in her changed appearance. 'Suddenly I can remember them all. *Magnifique*, *extraordinaire—incomparable*——' He made a mock gallic bow then turned to Nan to give her some chocolates. James Harvey was as nice as he looked. Fairlie wondered how he came to be working for Tate.

The evening was a success. The food was fine, the band romantic, the paintings good enough to look at all evening and James was an entertaining companion. His mock French accent had her giggling like a schoolgirl and confounded the true-blue French waiter. Fairlie talked about her coming exhibition and her fears for Bronwyn's early delivery and by the time he walked her up the front steps again they had achieved a camaraderie that even with Ben, had taken several nights like this.

'I enjoyed the evening, James. You're really very nice.' She reached up to kiss his cheek but found herself clasped in his arms instead.

'I'm not nice,' he whispered and took her kiss on his lips, binding her tight to him and moving his mouth on hers in brief ferocity. She stared at him when he let her go, straining to see his expression in the glow of the street light.

'Aren't you?'

He laughed in embarrassment. 'Sorry. But "nice" sounds so damned colourless.'

'Maybe I should say you are *extraordinaire* then,' she said lightly. 'Good night James.'

When he had gone, she closed the door and leaned against it. Why did some doubts niggle again about James? Nan was behaving oddly the next morning. She fussed and bustled as usual but her eyes kept sliding away from Fairlie's. When she sat down to drink her tea, her thumb was at her wedding ring, twisting it round and round.

'Would you like to ask Mr Van Lewin to Sunday night dinner?' she asked at last.

'If that suits you Nan. I'll 'phone him today.'

'Good. I'll clean the silver this week and starch my linen cloth—you know the one I embroidered before I was married . . .'

Fairlie regarded Nan's pink cheeks and excited air.

'All this fuss for someone you don't even know, Nan?' she teased and the old lady seemed rather flustered as she rescued a slice of toast from burning in her old, swing-door toaster.

Late that afternoon James sought Fairlie out with another invitation.

'A river cruise,' he smiled. 'I've got the use of a boat—just you and me and the city lights on the water. Sunday night. Will you come?'

Judging from his warm, sexy expression James had more in mind than looking at the city lights. Fairlie smiled and shook her head. 'Not Sunday night James. A friend of mine is coming to dinner.'

His face dropped. 'A friend?'

'That's right.'

'But couldn't you put it off? I might not be able to get—the boat again for a while.' He looked vaguely upset. Surely he wasn't jealous on the strength of one date?

'No. I 'phoned him today and he has already accepted.'

'Him?'

'Yes.' She was irritated by his insistence, as if he had some prior right. 'The man who is mounting my exhibition—I told you about him.'

'Does it have to be Sunday?' he asked again, taking her hand and turning imploring eyes on her. Rather shortly, she told him it did. He tried to shrug it off philosophically but did a poor job of it. She should be flattered, she supposed, that James wanted her company so much. But instead she was puzzled by the faint impression of strain in his easy manner as he said goodbye.

'About Sunday night,' Nan said after they had eaten dinner, 'would you mind if I asked someone else as well as Mr Van Lewin?'

'Of course not, Nan. Who did you have in mind— the Reynolds?'

'No . . .' Nan chewed her lip. 'It's Carson—I thought it would be nice if he came,' she hurried on at Fairlie's expression, 'and I've already invited him. Last night.'

'Invited—last night?' Fairlie said sharply. 'He was here last night while I was out?'

'Just after you left he dropped in. He stayed for hours and it was so pleasant. I had some of that cottage pie left and he had a bit and liked it so much that I said "wait until you try one of my baked dinners . . ." '

Of course he stayed for hours. He knew the coast was clear to have a long, persuasive talk to Nan, establishing his credentials as the pensioners' friend. With the meddling granddaughter out of the way with James, he could . . . Fairlie frowned. Had it been planned that way? James to distract her, keep her amused and away from home? No. She was being fanciful. And after all, Tate had accepted an invitation to dine here when she was present. On Sunday . . . Sunday about which James had been so persistent. Had she not already invited Pieter, she might well have gone cruising on the river leaving Carson Tate a clear field. Again.

'Tell me Nan, when you invited Mr Tate to dinner, did you say that you'd get me to bring along a friend as well—to make up a neat little dinner party?'

'Well—no, dear. I thought about inviting Mr Van Lewin later. I knew you wouldn't like the idea of Carson coming——'

'So you decided to break the news deviously?'

'Your Mr Van Lewin would even things up a bit——'

'And take the chill off the air, Nan?' Fairlie was thinking furiously. So that was the object of moving James the Nice in here. Tate had noticed the rapport between them at that first meeting and played on it, hoping to keep her occupied. Clever. While she was at work, James was here charming Nan and Tate himself was dropping by oozing pleasantries—a suspect enough habit for the Colossus chief executive—and when she came home James was always around in the nicest possible way. That only left the evenings and Mr Tate must have been very disappointed not to have been able to manipulate all those as well. But he'd made a start. That one night with James had been pleasant enough to start a trend. And James himself had confirmed it all. 'I'm not nice,' he had said during a pang of conscience after his delightful lies. Today he had been given his *next* assignment—to keep her out of the way on Sunday. No wonder he had looked dismayed when she'd refused.

'Where are you going dear?' Nan asked as Fairlie went purposefully to the door.

'I think I'd better clear up this matter of dinner with Mr Tate, Nan. After speaking with James I have a feeling that he might have a prior engagement.'

The tenth floor glowed in the night sky and Fairlie almost ran to the doors of the building. They were closed and she stood there, burning with fury and wondering whether she could get in via the basement carpark when a uniformed guard crossed the empty foyer and saw her. She hammered on the doors and he came cautiously over to them. When she showed no sign of stopping, he opened the door and listened to her demand to see Tate.

'Tell him it's Miss Jones.'

'Miss *Jones*,' he repeated with heavy irony.

'Yes, Jones. It isn't an alias. Let me in. I know he's up there. He always is until late every night so don't try fobbing me off.'

Reluctantly he 'phoned through, watching her as if she might be a subversive with a grenade. He couldn't realise just how much she wished she had something explosive with her, other than her temper.

'You can go up, Miss Jones,' he said in surprise and eyed her trim figure and massed, waving blonde hair with a new expression altogether. As she shot upwards in the life Fairlie smiled grimly. If he imagined she was a girlfriend of the boss, he was way off the mark.

The empty outer office worked its intimidation on Fairlie and she regretted now not delaying long enough to put on some make up. In the hushed, superior setting, her jeans, sweater and low heels seemed inadequate—as if she'd come to fight with no weapons. But she pushed open Tate's door and went in boldly. He was speaking on the 'phone, his shoulders relaxed into the high back of his chair his free arm raised, hand behind his head. At sight of her he came upright. Without pausing in his conversation, he nodded to her, eyes roving her figure and lingering on her loose, flyaway hair.

Once again she was forced to wait, to cool her heels and she flung away from the massive desk and his regard to the glass doors to the terrace. They slid open and she stepped out on to the tiled floor, crossing to the outer wall to look down on the city's towers and net of lights. Her gaze went to the pale gold that marked Nan's house below. It was no more than a speck in the darkness—only the verandah light she had left on and the glow from the lounge window delineated it. Her hands clenched and she walked along the thickly planted area which was dark save for the inner office lights filtering through branches and leaves. Inside Tate still lounged in his chair and she walked right to the end where the bar was set. She brushed the stems of a tall potted bamboo and it rustled. It was still swaying over her head when she turned to walk back to the doors.

Too late she saw her stupidity in coming out here to curb her impatience. The automatic doors swished open and Carson Tate joined her, his steps clicking on the ceramic floor. This was not where she would choose to speak to him—in a dim lit room hung with palm fronds and bamboo and the whole afloat against the dark winter sky.

'Good evening Fairlie. This is becoming a habit. But tonight your visit is an unexpected pleasure.'

'There will be no pleasure in it for you Mr Tate. I've come to tell you that your new underhanded scheme has come adrift.'

'Really?' he murmured. 'In that case I think I'll have a drink while I hear the worst. Join me?'

'I wouldn't join you in anything.'

'Rash words, Fairlie.' He went to the bar, switched on concealed lighting and mixed a drink. His face was underlit granite as he lifted the glass to his mouth. Then he switched off the lights and the glow from the office seemed dimmer suddenly.

'You are just about as low as they come aren't you? You've bamboozled Nan into letting you use the house and all the time it was a ruse to keep your man close, nibbling away at her resolution. And that wasn't all, was it Mr Tate? James—lovable, nice James has *other* useful qualities. What is he? Your tame gigolo whom you despatch when a woman enters the picture? Well I have news for you. Our delightful date last night is the last one, so you're back to square one. I'm still a problem on your hands. What *are* you going to do about me?'

There was a pause. He sounded amused. 'I've been thinking about that,' he said in a sexy voice.

'I suppose your offsider dashed to tell you that you won't have the field to yourself on Sunday when you have dinner with Nan. James did his best to tempt me with a boat cruise but he failed.'

'I had the impression you were rather partial to James.'

'Your protégé is a superb actor. He had me fooled for a while, but he's not my type.'

'Not enough man for you Fairlie?' he asked softly. She gasped in rage.

'Why you——' She lashed out as she tried to bypass him, but he grasped her arm and she was spun almost full circle.

'Let me go, you brute—are you going to add physical intimidation to your other off-colour tactics?' She struggled, all at once acutely afraid to be here with him. Holding her, he reached down and put his glass on a lacquered table and her hopes of escape were lost when he used both hands to restrain her.

'You're assuming a great deal, Fairlie—James' attraction to you is real, but he——'

'Let me go——' She wriggled some more but he held her fast.

'Listen to me you damned, suspicious little fool— James is acting on his own behalf, not mine——'

'Oh really? And while I was out with him, you dropped in for a cosy few hours of conversation alone with Nan. That's quite a coincidence.'

'That's all it was—a coincidence.'

'—and you had it all organised to have me out of the way on Sunday too—was that the night you hoped to get her signature? I suppose the papers are already drawn up with Sunday's date on them?'

He too was angry now. She could feel the anger flowing from his hands as he hauled her close, his fingers sinking into her upper arms. Alarmed at the jump of her senses, she put out her hands and pushed against his chest but even that served only to set her pulses hammering faster. Dismayed, humiliated, she felt her body respond. Her renewed struggles were against herself as much as him. Carson's hands moved from her shoulders to her wrists to hold off her blows. Curiously he watched her face.

'Where are those nerves of steel—are you afraid of me Fairlie?'

'Don't be a fool,' she snapped and shook him off. Or perhaps he merely decided to let her go. Whichever, she was glad to be rid of his touch. 'Of course I'm afraid of you. I'd be afraid of any man who had the Tate organisation behind him.' She backed off a pace.

'Forget the Tate organisation. You're afraid of *me*.'

She took another step back. Carson moved to regain the territory.

'No. Without the power of your family you're just another man Mr Tate.' If she said it often enough she might even believe that herself. He came towards her and she wavered, then moved backwards again. A philodendron leaf touched her hand and she jerked away from it.

'Then why are you backing off?' he asked softly.

'I'm not——' she denied even as she glanced behind her to see that she was running out of space.

The bamboo rustled, a palm leaf bobbed up and down as she brushed past. The night sky glowed with the city's phosphorescence, the office lighting shone muted through the screen of tropical foliage. It might as well be a jungle, Fairlie thought—and Carson Tate the hunter . . . the shadow play of bamboo danced on his face as he lengthened his stride to reach her. There

was nowhere to go. Behind her was the solidity of the
bar and she put out her arms each side of her to clutch
its edges. He stopped a stride away. For maybe half a
minute they stood there, looking at each other in the
leaf-spattered light and the city's nightglow. Carson
came no nearer but reached out and touched her hair.
Slowly his fingers slid into it. A slight contact, but one
that rocked her. Involuntarily her lips parted, her
breathing quickened. He let her hair fall again, ran his
fingertips down the side of her face. Along her jaw his
hand strayed, down her neck over the bones of her
shoulder then as she weakened at that featherlight
touch, he clasped her nape. Strongly he drew her to
him, sliding his other arm about her waist until she
was held close, breathing in his warmth and the smell
of him compounded of his day's work and the morning
scent of after-shave, lingering ... coffee, she thought
as he bent to her. He has had some coffee not long ago
... then his lips were on hers in the barest caress.
There and gone again. Around her his arms shifted,
closed more firmly and he kissed her again with a
tenderness that should have surprised her but didn't.
Her hands spread over his shoulders. She sighed, and
at the small sound he tightened his hold to a fierce
possessiveness and took advantage of her open lips to
ease his tongue between. Again he teased, explored,
withdrew the sweet, velvet intimacy only to renew it
when she pressed closer to him. She touched his hair
where it thicketed the cleft at the back of his head, ran
her hands over the bone and muscle of his back. Not
since Ben had she felt like this. Not since Ben had she
wanted to be loved ... for the first time she said his
name.

'Carson——' and there was pleasure and surprise in
her voice and as it trailed away, dismay too as if saying

that first name out loud had reminded her of the other. Tate. Carson Tate.

'Now we know,' he murmured and loosened his hold on her so that the cool air came flowing around, restoring sanity. 'I want you, Fairlie . . .'

And Carson Tate always got what he wanted. He wanted the house and he would get that—he wanted her too and she was actually making it easy for him. Because physically at least, she shared that want.

'. . . and I'm glad the feeling is mutual,' he whispered and bent to her again.

Her disgust was a bitter taste in her mouth and she whirled from his arms. The bamboo caught at her and sprang up again, swaying, rustling.

'Don't count on my reactions tonight, Mr Tate,' she snapped. 'You caught me off guard and you do have a certain expertise. But I'm not about to lose my head over mere technique.'

He didn't like that she could see, but though he stiffened he just murmured, 'And I thought we'd reached an understanding.'

'Don't bother turning up for dinner on Sunday night. You're not wanted Mr Tate.'

A smug smile. 'That wasn't my impression.'

'Just don't turn up.'

'I couldn't disappoint Nan.'

'Nan?' she echoed. 'You call her Nan?'

That smile again. Complacent, assured. It made her want to hit him.

'Didn't your grandmother tell you? We agreed that she will call me Carson and I will call her Nan.'

'But it's a family name——' Fairlie protested, hurt that this man, of all people, was allowed the same privilege that she had by blood.

'Just think of me as a cousin,' he suggested and

grabbed her wrist as she really did try to hit him. 'Tch, tch—mustn't get violent Fairlie. What would Nan say?' For long moments he held on to her as she strained an arm's length from him. 'You look so beautiful—I really don't want to let you go.'

'I think you should. Manhandling me won't endear you to my grandmother. She expects certain standards from those who call her "Nan".'

He laughed and let her go. 'Run along then Fairlie. I have too much work to get through anyway as it happens.'

'I hope it keeps you here all night.' She marched to the glass doors which opened with a shoosh.

As he followed her into the office he said drily, 'It might at that. You'll probably see my light on until after ten tonight,' he added with a half smile as if he knew that she often looked up at his bronzed strip of window-wall with its silhouetted palms and bamboo.

'I've better things to do than look at your lights.' She wrenched open the door.

'I sometimes look at yours,' he told her. 'Your bedroom is on the eastern side of the house, isn't it?'

'Oh, don't be so ridiculous,' she muttered and went headlong into Sandra's silent and deserted domain.

In the foyer the guard let her out, obviously intrigued by her ruffled appearance and bright cheeks. Nan too was interested. She asked a few predictable questions and Fairlie said she hadn't realised that Carson was as highly regarded as family and no, she hadn't really managed to clear up the matter of Sunday dinner. It seemed Carson had no previous engagement. And Nan, in a rare snub, told Fairlie that she could allow anyone she liked the privilege of calling her Nan. It was an ill wind . . . Fairlie thought, as she apologised and went to her room. She switched on her light.

'I sometimes look at yours,' he'd said. She turned it off again and found a book after fumbling about in the dark and took it into the lounge to read instead of curling up on her bed. Before she turned in she went, against all commonsense, out on to the landing and looked up at the Colossus building. It was ten-thirty and the strip of light still shone in his office. Fairlie went to her room and changed into her nightgown in the dark. She caught her hip on the old-fashioned chest of drawers. The throbbing pain of it brought tears to her eyes. All for nothing too she thought, furious with herself. The man on the tenth floor would not be standing at the window watching for her light.

'Damn you Carson Tate,' she whispered. 'Damn you.'

CHAPTER FIVE

IN the office the next day, Fairlie's mind whirled, going over last night. Even Bronwyn's cheery announcement that her husband had rushed her to hospital the night before in a false alarm failed to hold her attention for long. She called by at the gallery after work, ruefully recognising her reluctance to return to Nan's house where Carson might stroll in.

Pieter had re-framed some of her paintings. As they looked at them in his storeroom he said, 'You've travelled a long way forward with this series my sweet. But keep on with the journey. Your best is still to come—lurking there inside you.'

'Lurking, Pieter? That sounds unappetising.'

His laugh shook his patterned shirt. 'Talking of appetites——'

'Which we weren't . . .'

Pieter waved away her impertinence. 'What time would your grandmama like me to come to dinner on Sunday?'

'Around seven I think.'

'Something the matter, Fairlie?'

Carson Tate as a dinner guest all night, that was the matter. 'Nothing——' She smiled. Pieter could sense something on her mind as easily as he could identify the herbs in a gourmet sauce. 'Nan might have another guest on Sunday Pieter, but it's not definite.' He was watching her still and she forced a light-heartedness she was far from feeling. 'I'm looking forward to seeing you then Pieter . . . and that reminds me, I

83

must find some timber to brace one of Nan's dining chairs.'

'Brat,' he said, taking her hand to bend his bulk over it. The touch of his lips was scant and brief. 'Wear your hair down for me fairest,' he said and flicked her chin with a hefty forefinger.

Nan's gates were standing open when she drove up. Both gates. It was several seconds before she saw the significance of it and steered the car to the garage under the house, on the tracks that Pa had used years ago. Then she went to inspect the rusted, immovable bolt to discover that it had been replaced by a new one and the corresponding slot in the concrete reamed out.

'Carson had it attended to,' Nan told her when she went inside. 'It's good to have a man about, isn't it?'

'Is it?'

'Now, Fairlie, you must thank him for that.'

'Yes. I must.'

'Really, dear, Carson is bending over backwards to help us and you can hardly spare him the time of day. You're a lovely girl but inclined to be unforgiving.' She paused. 'About your father for instance . . .'

'What about him, Nan?'

'Try to understand him, Fairlie. He writes to me every Christmas you know and always asks about you. Don't you think you could bring yourself to write to him just once?'

'He's never in one place long enough . . .' she said unconvincingly.

'I know you were hurt when he behaved the way he did after your mother died—that other woman and the drinking. I was hurt myself at the time but now I can't believe it was because he felt no grief. Just the opposite. He went a little crazy I suppose.'

Fairlie's mouth set. 'Then he just left to drift

around like some nomad as if he had no one else. And I was there.'

'Write to him, dear—please. I don't condone everything he's done but he loves you dearly. He only went away because—oh, I suppose because he was empty of anything to give you.'

Nan's words hung in her mind and brought visions of her father in times when he had plenty to give. Maybe he had been playing the clown to hide his grief. Maybe he had to leave or lose his sanity. After a while she took a pad and pen and began to write. It was difficult, her emotions scattered as they were by the turn in her relationship with Carson and now by guilt kicked off by a few poignant words. Fairlie left the letter unfinished and went to the kitchen.

James was there, laughing with Nan but he sobered when he received no answering smile from Fairlie. She busied herself peeling potatoes for their evening meal and remained outside the conversation. The potatoes sliced into the pan with angry clunks and she topped them up with a gush of water that nearly floated them away.

'Can I see you for a minute?' James asked when she'd finished. His pleasant face was apologetic, guilty. In the gleaming hallway he said, 'I suppose you found out. Did Carson tell you?'

'Not in so many words, James. But I rather got the picture. You certainly put on a super act.'

'Act?' He shook his head. 'I don't know what you mean. Except for the lies of course.'

'It's the lies I'm talking about,' she snapped. 'Don't you think you deserve better than to act as Tate's tame gigolo?'

James stared at her, a frown drawing his fair brows together. 'Gigolo?'

'Well, he gave you the assignment, didn't he? Told you to win me over and take me out to give him a clear field with Nan? Why else were you so embarrassed when he was standing there watching you make arrangements for dinner the other night and why else would you be *so* disappointed that I couldn't make a date with you for Sunday? Because you knew the boss wouldn't like it. He wanted me out of the way so that he could ingratiate himself with Nan——' She finished with a great deal more heat than she'd started with. The moment Carson came into it, her temper went sky high.

James looked at her oddly. 'I thought you said he'd told you——' He hesitated, then, 'Oh, it's no good. I might as well tell you. My conscience is too damned punishing. Fairlie, I'm engaged to be married. That's why I was embarrassed with Carson watching the other day. He knows I'm engaged and stayed there to try and make me back down—and if I seemed insistent about Sunday it was because I'd told a dozen lies to Debra about going out with the boys, so that I could be free. When you said you couldn't come it was all in vain. I felt guilty——'

'You mean—Carson didn't tell you to distract me?'

He took her hands. 'No of course not. In fact he didn't like the idea of me seeing you at all—but I just couldn't resist—you're so, well—different from Debra. Don't get me wrong, she's a fantastic girl, threw up her job to come up here when I was posted and I've never even looked at another woman. Until you. I'm sorry . . .'

Fairlie was dumbfounded. All those fiery accusations she'd hurled at Carson. She remembered now him saying something sarcastic about 'another engagement' to James as they discussed their dinner plans, a tongue-in-cheek reminder that he wasn't free. James' subsequent embarrassment had seemed perfectly natural. Carson's goading she had put down to his shrewd wish to make her sympathise with James, to push them closer together. It was all a mistake—*not* careful, mercenary planning. She pulled her hands free.

'So I was just a casual fling before you got married was I James?' she said, thinking of Ben. She had not only played the part of faithful fiancée—now she had nearly been the 'other girl' too. But it was easier to take strangely enough, than the idea that Carson had arranged it.

'Fairlie—I—I——' he stammered and she took pity on him.

In James' case it probably *was* just a single lapse and not one of many that made Ben's affairs a habit.

'Let's forget it James. It's nice to know that you weren't acting—but not so good to know that you were chatting me up while you were engaged.'

'Fairlie, it wasn't just—I mean—a physical thing. I really like you a lot. If we'd met sooner . . .'

'Oh, for heaven's sake, let's not get into a scene from *Casablanca*, James,' she said in irritation, then at the sight of his suffused, guilty face added, 'Or you might start using that atrocious French accent of yours.'

James laughed regretfully. '*Magnifique*,' he said.

'Something's bothering James,' Nan said over dinner. 'I do hope he's not coming down with something.'

Just a mild case of infidelity, Fairlie thought but said nothing. James could break the news to Nan that he was soon to be married. And he would be rapped rather smartly over the knuckles then she guessed.

'And Carson has something on his mind too. He came by this afternoon. I think he was hoping to speak to you.'

She saw him the next morning. In fact she almost walked into him as she went out the back to empty the tea pot on Nan's parsley. He steadied her with a hand on her arm and looked down at her gravely.

'Good morning, Fairlie.'

'Hello, Carson.' She looked up at him and saw the flicker of surprise as she used his name. 'Thank you for having the gate fixed.'

He smiled. 'It's a pleasure.'

'I believe I owe you an apology . . .'

He raised an eyebrow and his grey eyes moved slowly over her face. There was a mild morning ray of sunshine slanting in through the back door where he had just entered and it highlighted the flecks of silver in his dark hair, gilded the collar of his shirt and jacket and one wide shoulder. Some new, alert part of her brain registered the lines under his eyes. The big man had an air of weariness about him. Was it because he had been working late so often? Last night his office lights had been on until nearly ten.

'. . . about James. I thought you had given him me as an assignment—to distract me, get me out of the way while you . . .' It sounded absolutely stupid now, she realised.

'While I worked on Nan? You don't know me very well.' His grey eyes glinted. 'For a start, I'd never give someone else an—assignment—that I knew I could handle better myself.'

She stepped away from him. 'Don't count on it.'

He caught her arm just above the wrist. 'I was joking, Fairlie. The other night was purely selfish. It had nothing to do with Colossus or anything else. I hope you believe that.'

'Frankly I'm not interested in that. All I know is that you want something and you'll do whatever you can to get it.'

'Now *that* you can believe, Fairlie.'

'I meant the land.'

'Of course. So did I. What else?' he murmured in amusement. Another of those raking looks and he bent his head and kissed her. She was too startled to move away, she told herself after he had gone. He was too quick for her to sidestep, she rationalised as she emptied the tea-leaves with a shaking hand. The sound of his voice in the office with James murmured all through her breakfast. She listened for that voice the next morning before she went to work and in the afternoon. But Carson didn't call.

'He's away,' Nan told her when she probed casually for the information. 'Just for a couple of days. He'll be back on Sunday.'

'So he's still coming to dinner?'

'Yes and he 'phoned from Melbourne to ask if he could bring someone with him.'

A peculiar sensation assailed Fairlie. 'Who?'

'He didn't say—he was in a hurry and of course I said that was fine with me. He sounded worried about something.'

'He's got a cheek if you ask me,' Fairlie said indignantly. 'To include his girlfriend at the last minute like that.'

She paced about the kitchen in agitation. Geraldine Hallam she supposed, Pieter's choosy customer, which probably meant she was one of those well-heeled, over-groomed women with aristocratic looks and triple row of pearls. Yes, a woman like that would look rather suitable on Carson's arm. Elegant but small and clinging—complete femininity as a foil to his sock-you-in-the-eye masculinity. Nan was unperturbed about an extra guest but Fairlie went to her room, irritated more than she liked at the thought of Carson coming here with his girlfriend.

On Saturday she and Nan went through the house with dusters and polish until every surface shone. Nan's precious worn Persian rug glowed beneath the cedar dining table. Her crystal glasses were set out on the old mahogany sideboard and the cutlery, polished during the week was arrayed in readiness. It was an event for Nan and Fairlie squashed her own misgivings about the evening to give full rein to her grandmother's enjoyment.

On Sunday night Nan wore a new dress. She fussed over her jewellery and finally decided upon the single string of pearls given to her by Pa on one of their forty-five anniversaries. She was a pastel portrait. Ivory, pink—blue. Fairlie elected to eschew jewellery altogether. She wasn't going to compete with Geraldine Hallam on *that* score. The selective thought astonished her. She pulled on her dress telling herself that she didn't wish to compete with her on *any* score. Even so, as she patted the low necked sea-green dress over her figure she was pleased. The colour suited her well, bringing out the green in her eyes. The soft flounce around the neck was feminine without being fussy and her loose hair provided a shining honey foil for the texture of the fabric. At the last moment she caught up her hair with gold slides at each side.

'Oh Fairlie, you look lovely. So feminine,' Nan approved, then waggishly, 'He won't be able to take his eyes off you.'

'I don't care if he looks my way at all,' Fairlie retorted.

'But dear—surely—I mean he's showing your paintings and everything.' Nan looked closer at her granddaughter's rising colour.

'Oh. Pieter. I thought you meant——' Fairlie caught Nan's eye and cursed herself for the revealing statement. 'Was that someone at the door Nan?'

'Not yet, dear, but I think I heard a car.'

Fairlie lingered at the tilted old-fashioned mirror when she heard Nan greet Carson. She waited a moment longer for the sound of another female voice but heard none. At last she moved and went to the open doors of the lounge mentally prepared for the sight of Carson with an elegant woman at his side. But she wasn't immediately visible. Carson was. He was tall and dominating in the room—his strong throat bared by an open necked blue shirt worn with slacks and blazer. Fairlie stood in the doorway watching for a moment as he smiled down at Nan—then he turned his head and saw her. As their eyes met she felt a jolt that set the earth quaking beneath her feet and it was all she could do to summon the polite smile she had prepared.

'Good evening, Fairlie,' he smiled and came over to her capturing her in the doorway. 'You look beautiful tonight. I see you didn't blister,' he added *sotto voce* and studied her cleavage quite openly. There were blotches there still, pale but masked by a smear of make up.

'It's hardly the time to be ogling me, surely.'

'Name the time Fairlie and I'll do more than ogle.'

'There isn't a calendar with *that* date on it, Carson.' She ignored his low laugh. 'And you must be an even bigger rat than I thought to talk like this when your girlfriend is with you.'

'Is that what's bothering you? Let me introduce you to my "girlfriend".'

He moved and so did Nan and she had her first glimpse of Carson's friend.

'This is my son David, Fairlie. David, meet Miss Jones.'

His son. It shouldn't be a surprise. James had said he had a son. But Fairlie was confounded to be suddenly faced with a boy instead of femininity and a triple row of pearls. He was perhaps thirteen, not especially big, though Fairlie searched her memory for an idea of size to age ratio and could find none. He had a young-old look about him as if his face had not yet decided between boy and adolescent but it was clear that he would one day look like his father. The similarity was there in the as-yet unconfirmed squareness of the jaw, in the strongly marked brows and the thick, dark hair.

He put out his hand. 'How do you do, Miss Jones.'

She collected her wits and smiled. 'Hello, David.' The handshake was brief and cool. The boy's blue eyes that flicked up at her were hostile though not, she felt, necessarily at her. A wealth of resentment simmered in their depths and Fairlie kept her smile and looked at his father. The lines she had noticed about Carson's eyes were deeper and there was an odd new quality to his strong face which she couldn't pin down. But she might be imagining it she admitted, as he seated himself, accepted a drink and made light conversation with his usual aplomb. David took a seat and stared into his Coke. Fairlie followed Carson's eyes to where his son sat in the chair that was the furthest one possible from him.

'Well now, this *is* a surprise,' Nan said, 'Fairlie thought you would be bringing a——' she glanced at

David, 'that is, when you said you wanted to bring someone else she thought . . .'

Carson smiled over his drink. 'Jumping to conclusions again, Fairlie?'

'It was an obvious one,' she retorted. 'I don't imagine you think I've invited a *girl*friend to dinner tonight?'

'Point taken,' he said and watched her as she left the room in summons to the front doorbell. It was Pieter.

'Pieter, how good to see you,' she said and kissed his cheek.

'Fairlie, my darling, you look like a sea nymph. I hardly dare touch you—you might shatter into seafoam.'

She laughed, aware that his booming voice would be clearly heard by the others.

'These are for you, my lovely,' he put a dozen exquisite white roses in her arms and brandished an enormous box of chocolates, 'and these are for your grandmama.'

His entrance was spectacular. Nan's eyes grew round as Pieter's midnight blue velvet jacket filled the doorway. They grew rounder as he advanced on her with his strangely graceful gait and kissed her hand.

'Well!' she kept saying, and, 'Mr Van Lewin, you shouldn't,' when he presented her with the chocolates. Pieter worked his considerable charm on her and while she dimpled and laughed at his outrageously extravagant speech, Carson got up and strolled over to Fairlie. His lips twitched as he looked from Pieter to her. 'Maybe this is a case of *too* much man.'

Loyalty to Pieter put a sparkle in her eyes.

'Is there such a thing as too much generosity, too much culture, too much integrity, Carson?'

He looked down at the drink in his hand, back at

her. 'I beg your pardon. I made the joke without thinking.' Which surprised her so much that Nan had to perform the rest of the introductions.

The evening was totally unlike Fairlie's expectations. Pieter filled one end of the table and took on the job of carving with Dickensian relish. The roasts looked tiny set before his midnight blue magnificence.

'Thank goodness we got two,' Nan said in an aside to Fairlie. Carson opened the wine and poured it. Nan smiled as the men performed the traditional male duties. David politely passed the vegetable platter to her and she sighed.

'It's wonderful to have three men about the house.'

'Mrs Holborn, I object,' Pieter bellowed with good humour. 'I *alone* amount to two men.'

Even David smiled at that, though Fairlie noticed that as he met his father's gaze he lapsed into sulkiness again.

'Yes, when Fairlie said that you were *twice* the man that Carson is, I just thought she was being—oh! I mean——' Nan flushed in embarrassment.

'You thought I was being insulting about Carson as usual,' Fairlie finished for her and slanted a defiant glance at Carson—'So I was. Carson knows what I think of him Nan, and it doesn't bother him one bit.' She saw David's head come up at that. He looked quite interested.

Carson directed a soulful look at her. 'On the contrary, Fairlie—every time you visit my office to tell me what's on your mind, I'm left feeling very— bothered.'

Blandly he poured more wine.

'Superb, Nan,' he said later as they finished the meal.

'Superb?' Pieter repeated gustily. 'Nothing so pallid. *Magnificent*, Madam!'

There was a pleased protest from Nan.

'Sumptuous,' from Carson.

'*Ambrosial,*' from Pieter.

Then a pause.

'I rest on ambrosial,' Carson declared, and Pieter laughed.

Their gentle jousting went on all evening with the honours about equal. The wit and matched anecdotes almost seemed some sort of competition. A natural male search for dominance over the group, Fairlie supposed. But every now and then, when she expected Carson to deliver a coup, he would courteously give the advantage to Pieter. She watched Carson surreptitiously, forced to admire his ease and manners. But now and then his eyes would move to his son and his urbanity would slip a fraction. In turn Fairlie became aware that she too was being observed. Pieter's shrewd, blue eyes found her often and once he raised a blond brow at her acid-sweet manner to the Colossus chief. When Nan's homely pudding had been disposed of, when the last scrap of custard and brandy butter had been eulogised by Pieter, they moved into the lounge.

'Pieter, I love your jacket,' Fairlie said as he lowered himself into a sturdy thirty-year old armchair.

'It is rather delightful, isn't it?' He brushed the lapels with one large hand. 'I ordered the material to re-cover a chaise longue actually, but I liked it so much I had it made into a jacket.' He paused while everyone laughed. 'Of course, I had to order a little extra fabric for the jacket.'

David guffawed at that but stopped when his father looked over. Nan talked to the boy and he responded in a friendly fashion but lapsed into monosyllables when Carson joined in. It was peculiar, Fairlie thought, to see Carson out of his depth at last. Because that was clearly how it was. His son was doing his very best to ignore him completely. She watched Carson's irritation grow and when it smouldered into anger at David's polite unsociability, she hurried to avert the inevitable.

'David,' she said with authority in her voice, 'will you do me a favour?' The boy shrugged and got up to follow her. 'You wouldn't mind helping with the washing up, would you?' she said in the kitchen and he shrugged again.

'Sure. Don't you have a dishwasher?' he asked, looking around Nan's old kitchen.

She laughed. 'Not usually. But tonight we do.' She presented him with the plug and the sponge. 'You.'

He grinned. 'When I've washed them, do I stack the dishes here, Miss Jones?' he said after he had completed the interesting business of whipping up enough detergent froth for the job. Fairlie wondered at what age that lost its fascination.

'Yes. Call me Fairlie, David.'

'Fairlie. That's unusual.'

'It's a kind of pet name for Felicity,' she told him. 'That was my mother's name.'

'Is she dead?' he wanted to know and she nodded. 'Mine's divorced—well, from my father anyway. She's married again now.'

'So I heard.' Fairlie had been intending to leave the boy to it and return to the lounge, but now she picked up a tea cloth and began to wipe the suds-coated dishes. 'I think you might have been a bit heavy-handed with the detergent, David.'

He grinned again. 'But that's the best part.'

'Yes, I suppose it is. So—it's not much fun having divorced parents?'

He gave her a funny look and didn't answer.

'Well, you're not making much secret of it,' she went on. 'Don't you get along with your Dad?'

'No. He doesn't really want me around. But he wouldn't let me stay with Grandad. Mum's gone overseas with Greg—that's her new husand. He's in politics.'

'What makes you think your father doesn't want you?'

David looked at her with the resigned face of an adult. 'I just know. I suppose I can tell you I don't even like him without shocking you. *You* don't like him either. Most people can't imagine anyone disliking their own father.'

The words stabbed at Fairlie. She thought of her unfinished letter. 'Why don't you like him?'

'Why don't you?' he came back.

'I suppose—I feel your father and I have a conflict of interests,' she said carefully, striving to be scrupulously fair. 'He wants to build a car park on this spot and Nan wants to stay living here. It bothers me.'

'Why do you have him to dinner then?'

'Because—nothing is ever all black or all white I suppose. It is possible to hate one thing about someone but to find other things that are——' she paused, conscious of the irony in the words,'—okay. Besides,' she finished, 'Nan likes your Dad and it's her house.'

'Well, that's the real reason he's here then, isn't it?'

Fairlie pulled a face at him. 'You're a chip off the old block all right.'

'No, I'm not. I don't want to be like him any more.

He never made much effort to come and see me—he even forgot my birthdays.'

'That surprises me.'

'Why?'

'Even if he forgot himself, his secretary wouldn't.'

'His *secretary*?' David looked askance at her.

'Oh sure. I've worked for busy men like your father. One of my jobs was to remind them of birthdays and anniversaries.'

David wiped lather from his shirt. 'His didn't do a very good job then.'

It was on the tip of her tongue to ask him what his mother said when his birthdays went unmarked by his father, but decided it really was none of her business. Carson had to make his own defence to his son. Amazingly she was by no means convinced that Carson *would* forget his boy's birthdays.

'Anyway, I don't like the way he does things,' David went on after a minute. 'Knocking things down and bulldozing trees and stuff just for another big building. He only thinks of money. The environment counts for nothing with him.'

She laughed. 'That's a funny thing for a Tate to say. Your grandfather and great uncles started the business by knocking things down and building others. Do you disapprove of them too?'

'He's the one who runs Colossus.'

'Well, give him time. He hasn't been running it for long.' What am I saying? Fairlie listened to herself in astonishment. David's face was sombre. 'Does he know you're a conservationist—a greenie?' she teased, trying to get a smile from him.

'Nah. We don't talk much.'

'Hmm. I had noticed.' She folded up the tea-towel. 'That's about it, David. Thanks a lot.' She held up the almost empty detergent bottle. 'I must remember to buy some more of this tomorrow. Bio-degradable, of course.'

He dried his hands and laughed. 'I'm not *that* fanatic, Fairlie.'

'Not fanatic about what?' Carson said from the door and David turned away immediately.

'Nothing.'

'We were talking about detergent,' Fairlie said. 'And conservation, David is concerned about the environment.'

'Is that so? We must talk about it sometime, David.' Carson smiled at his son's back.

'What would you know about it?' There was dead silence but for the delicate popping of lathery bubbles left sliding down the sink.

'Oh, I've come up against both sides of the problem. You might find some of it pretty interesting.' The cords on Carson's neck were standing out. Fairlie stared in fascination at the evidence of his restraint.

'Don't bet on it.'

The rude reply echoed into a silence.

'Shall we go back inside?' Fairlie suggested, eager to escape the gathering tension between the two Tates. David went promptly and his father's eyes followed him with such a raw expression that Fairlie nearly put out her hand to him in consolation. But Carson looked back at her with icy calm.

'You've done a little probing, I suppose, Fairlie, over the dishes. Fished for details of my divorce that so interested you? I hope you've derived some pleasure from turning over the ashes.'

The attack took her by surprise. An acid reply sprang to mind but she saw that it was possible she was receiving the overspill of his frustration and though she followed him, indignant, from the kitchen, she remained silent.

Later, as Carson and David made their departure, followed by Pieter, Fairlie examined a hitherto rare feeling. A maternal one. And as if that wasn't enough, this new feeling was as much for the man as for his son.

But maternal feelings lingered only briefly. When Fairlie arrived home one day the following week to find surveyors along Nan's boundaries she quite forgot those tantalising glimpses of vulnerability in Carson Tate. For some reason the sight of the tripods inside Nan's garden upset her more than they would have done a week before. Had she become soft in the head to actually expect better things of the man? Her flare of temper astounded the surveyors who packed up post haste and left.

This time she resisted the urge to confront Carson in person. Instead she 'phoned him from James' office and after a half minute wait, heard his rough, deep voice.

'You're anticipating things aren't you, Mr Tate?'

'It's "Mister" again now, is it?'

'After that little outburst of yours at dinner here I should think it would be. For your information I was *not* pumping your son about you or your ex-wife, merely asking him about himself. David is a very nice, articulate boy.'

There was silence. Stiffly he said, 'I'd had a trying few days. I apologise if I took my feelings out on you.'

'There was no *if* about it.'

'All right, all right. I've apologised,' he said in a driven tone. 'And what am I anticipating that has made you 'phone me?'

'Moving Nan out. Just don't rush ahead with your plans—sending in the surveyors is too hasty by far.'

'Fairlie—sending in the surveyors is nothing new. Your grandmother's boundaries which, I might remind you, are also ours, have been surveyed before. But this time I'm trying to——'

'As long as they stay on *your* land. They were on Nan's today. If it happens again I'll regard it as trespassing.'

'Once—just once, I wish you'd let me finish saying something,' he muttered. 'That's all is it, Fairlie?' he went on in a steely tone. 'I am rather busy. If you have any more petty complaints would you speak to James about them? You remember James—my offsider and sometime gigolo?'

She slammed the 'phone down.

It was too much of a coincidence that the pavement in front of the house was gouged into jagged piles of asphalt and soil the following afternoon. Fairlie parked her car in the street and viewed the impassable drive with hands on hips. So—the intimidation tactics were in full swing again. No sooner had she become used to the luxury of workable gates and a garage, than some new inconvenience rendered them useless.

'You pig, Carson Tate,' she said under her breath and tossed a glowering look at the bronze-glassed tenth floor.

'Hello, Fairlie.'

She spun around to find David Tate at her side— clad in a school uniform and cap and carrying a bulging sports bag.

'Oh, David,' she blinked, taken aback to find him there while she mumbled insults about his father. 'What are you doing here?'

'There's no bus from my school to the flat so I have

to come here——' he indicated the Colossus building
with a toss of his head, 'I suppose the firm chopped up
your entrance.'

'I suppose so.'

'It's typical.' The boy shrugged. It seemed to be his
favourite non verbal communication. Except for his
very speaking sulks in his father's presence.

'It's council property, so I suppose the firm must
have a permit for the work. And they wouldn't be
allowed to do anything that was unnecessary.' It was
irksome, but she had to admit that in the effort to be
unprejudiced for David's benefit, she had lost the fine
fury of indignation. And a little fine fury in reserve for
Carson seemed a very desirable thing. A safe thing.

When she took her bag from the car, David was still
standing there looking a little lost.

'Would you like to come in for a drink, David?' she
asked. 'Will your father be expecting you?'

'Oh, he won't know if I'm there or not. I'll just sit
about in one of the offices until he finishes work I
expect. I'd like to come in if it's all right with Mrs
Holborn.'

'Sure.' Fairlie said and as they skirted the
devastated footpath and drive and walked up the path
together she wondered if Carson was watching from
his window on the tenth floor.

CHAPTER SIX

NAN greeted the boy with pleasure and offers of refreshment. She produced husky slices of fruit cake and a large glass of milk which David downed in seconds.

'I know what appetites you young men have,' Nan said showering cookies on to a plate. Fairlie saw a little casual prying coming up. Sure enough her grandmother settled down at the table with David and went on. 'I suppose your mother feeds you up when you get home from school.'

'She isn't always there. She's a consultant. Interior decorating. She has her own showrooms and everything. That was how she met Greg.'

'Did she decorate his house for him?'

David disposed of a mighty mouthful of cookie. 'Yeah. He's got a great house—right on the coast. Greg's going to give me a room with a sea view.'

'So you'll live with your mother again when she comes back——' Nan prodded. 'When will that be?'

'About two months. I wish they were back now.'

'Still, it will be fun for you being with your father,' Nan said with a hint of reproof.

'Greg's going to stand as a Member of Parliament,' David said, choosing another cookie and doggedly ignoring Nan's comment about his father. 'He's going to speak out about conservation and protecting the country from multi-national companies and—and others. He says it's time for them to give for a change instead of just taking. Greg says . . .'

His 'Greg says' had overtones of defensiveness, Fairlie couldn't help thinking.

'Greg sounds very articulate,' she commented. 'But then he'd have to be if he wants to succeed in politics. Your father seems to agree with Greg about big business doesn't he?' David looked puzzled. 'I mean Colossus must provide a few hundred jobs and it sponsors all sorts of sporting events and scholarships.'

She saw Nan raise her brows. It *was* a turnabout. David was forcing her to abandon her own absolute prejudice in the face of his own.

'He only does that for the publicity. Greg says it's cheaper for companies to give out prize money than to pay for image advertising.'

Greg seemed to say a lot and little of it in favour of the boy's father. Why did David's mother allow that to happen—especially as she herself had no doubt enjoyed the benefits of being part of the Tate empire.

She asked David about school which made a change from 'Greg says'. David was non-committal but as he was already a member of the tennis squad and a cricket team reserve, it seemed he had settled in rather well. Fairlie finished her tea thoughtfully while Nan took David to the spare bedroom to show him Pa's collection of war memorabilia.

'Wow, Mrs Holborn's got a Japanese bayonet and an old rifle with a wooden stock,' he said when they came back. 'I've only seen them in the War Museum.'

'That's a bloodthirsty look you're wearing, David,' Fairlie observed. 'For a conservationist and greenie, that is.'

He grinned. 'Well—I don't agree with war and killing—but this is *history* isn't it?'

'I see—a purely educational interest is it?'

'That's it,' he nodded, perfectly serious and she laughed. He looked so much like a smaller Carson in that mock-teasing mood he adopted to annoy her. Except that David didn't annoy her at all.

'As I said—a chip off the old block, David Tate.'

'Don't call me that. I'm going to change my name when Mum and Greg come back,' he blurted, one hand fidgeting with his school cap that lay on the table. Nan tut-tutted.

'Yes I would,' Fairlie said mildly. ' "David" is nice but quite commonplace I suppose. What were you considering—Alvin—Sholto? Marmaduke has a certain ring to it.'

The passionate look died from David's eyes and he grinned. Then he laughed out loud. 'That's not what I mean and you know it. Sholto.' He laughed again. 'Is that really a name?'

'Oh Carson,' exclaimed Nan and they looked around to see him in the kitchen doorway. 'Come in and have some tea. David dropped in on his way up to see you and . . .' Her words ran out as Carson failed to respond. His eyes were on his son's face. David's laughter had cut off as if by a switch and his head dropped forward in sulky closure.

'I'll go and get my bag,' he muttered in reply to his father's greeting. Nan hurried after him, shaking her head at this estrangement between father and son. 'You can borrow that book I showed you about the first war David——' she was saying as they went along the hall.

Carson eyed Fairlie in silence. Her sympathies were temporarily with him in the face of his son's rejection, but so searching were his eyes that any softer feelings were banished in favour of self-defence. She remembered the unusable driveway.

'You give with one hand and take away with the other, don't you Carson?'

His eyes narrowed. 'This is leading to something I suppose, Fairlie. Why not just come to the point?'

'Now that the gate's fixed, the driveway is impassable. Is it some sort of physchological game you play?'

'I'm playing no games. None that you don't like anyway.'

Her face warmed. 'Stop harassing us. Sending surveyors around and blocking the driveway won't get you what you want, I can promise you that. While ever Nan wants to stay in this house, I'll fight tooth and nail for her right to refuse you.'

'Tooth and nail?' He grinned. 'That could be interesting. But there's no need to fight on your grandmother's behalf. Keep your nails sharpened for another fight—if you must make a battle of it.'

'There is only one fight between us Carson and I can call on more weapons than you think.'

'Going to bring in the press after all, Fairlie?' He looked amused at the idea and her blood pressure soared. 'What are you going to use against me? Complain that I have installed a high ranking executive as liaison officer between Nan and the site crew for her protection? Paid her handsomely for the use of her house and services—fixed her gate—given her a new lease of life? Face it Fairlie,' his voice dropped to a smiling, sexy tone—, '—whatever the fight you've nothing to use against me.'

Involuntarily she looked down at David's cap. She picked it up from the table. There was instant tension in Carson's face. The school cap twirled on her finger.

'Haven't I?' she asked.

His face contorted in rage and she stepped back,

afraid for one moment that he might actually strike her.

'You bitch,' he bit out.

'Now you know what it feels like to be helpless, Carson,' she taunted, driven on by his contempt. How dared he label her names when he was prepared to use his massive weapons to remove Nan from his path? 'There are some things even *your* money can't get for you . . .' Her voice died away at the brief glimpse of pain in his eyes and she wished the words recalled immediately. So that was why he had been angry that other time—'trying to weasel your way into people's affections——' she had said and it had hurt him unintentionally. Fairlie cursed herself for this more deliberate blow. She would never dream of using the very tenuous friendship between herself and David against the boy's father. Only frustration had made her even suggest such a thing.

'Look Carson, I didn't mean——' she began when Nan came back followed by David who had his bag and the book from Nan's shelves.

'Goodbye Mrs Holborn, Fairlie——' David said in the subdued voice he used in his father's presence.

'The name is Jones,' Carson snapped. 'Miss Jones.'

'But she asked me to call her Fairlie,' David protested, actually lifting his head to argue. Carson stared down stonily at him—

'Miss Jones.'

With resentment David re-phrased his farewell and Fairlie bit her lip. What had she done now?

'Can I come by tomorrow?' David asked her and she hesitated, conscious of Carson's freezing stare.

'Um—well—of course.'

'No. You can't,' his father broke in and clapped a hand to David's shoulder, turning him to the door. But Nan wouldn't hear of such an embargo. David was more than welcome she declared, ignoring Carson's stony expression. She bustled to the door with them and Carson relented, unable to resist her. Nan had a power of her own and it was ironic that Carson should fall victim to it. Fairlie just wished she hadn't demeaned herself by pretending she would try to widen the rift between father and son. She had no opportunity to retract and as a result spent a good deal of time tossing in her bed that night regretting her hasty words.

'You look a bit peaky—everything all right at work dear?' Nan asked a few days later.

'Fine. Mr Elliott's report is coming along nicely and Bronwyn's had a second false alarm. I won't get in the lift with her anymore.'

'Are you worried about your exhibition?' Nan persisted. 'You look dark under the eyes.'

'No, Pieter has that well in hand. There will be quite a crowd for the opening.'

'That's lovely, dear. And I'm sure I'm going to love it. James is going he tells me.'

'Yes, I asked Pieter to invite him—and a friend.'

'A friend?' Nan said, surprised. 'I thought maybe you'd invited him as your partner——'

Fairlie smiled. So James had postponed his confession about Debra. 'No. James is nice but not my type, Nan.'

'You're probably right. He's a bit *too* nice for you Fairlie.'

'Nan, that sounds unflattering.'

'All I meant was that you want someone a bit stronger than James—someone as strong or stronger than yourself.'

'I've given up trusting men, Nan. Maybe I don't want one at all.'

'It's a terrible thing not to trust, Fairlie.'
'Or to trust too much, Nan.'

Pieter's opening was impeccably organised. The wine was excellent of course, and the guests for the main chosen as carefully as Pieter would select a menu and divided into three groups—possible buyers, hyphenated names for the social pages, photographer and friends. Fairlie was early and showed Nan the thirty large canvases that made up the exhibition.

'Well I never,' she said once or twice, obviously searching for a good, serviceable, non-committal comment. And to Pieter's suppressed horror she admitted to seeing a French poodle in the centre of one of Fairlie's series of four 'astral' paintings.

James Harvey turned up rather self-consciously and introduced his fiancée to Nan and Fairlie. Debra was small and clung to James. She was ultra-feminine, a little helpless and every bit as nice as he was. Perhaps, Fairlie thought, James had wanted a temporary break away from 'nice' with a woman who had the nerve to drive a Colossus earthmover.

'Gracious,' cried Nan, 'how long have you been engaged James?'

It was Debra who volunteered that it had been three months and soon after when the girl was momentarily diverted, Fairlie heard Nan say to James: 'That was naughty of you James. Let's have no more of that.'

He was considerably chastened to be on the receiving end of Nan's old-fashioned disapproval. Fairlie gave him a wink as she went her way to do duty with the guests. But James and thoughts of anything else were driven from her head when she saw Carson's dominant figure in a group around Pieter. Carson— here?

She immediately turned and moved in the opposite direction, seeking out someone, anyone who could keep her legitimately occupied and out of Carson's range. Her last meeting with him loomed in her mind and filled her with both anger and guilt and she needed a few moments to decide on her approach to him. An apology of course, she owed him that.

'It's not like you to turn and run Ms Jones,' a familiar sarcastic voice said behind her and she realised her few moments had run out. She looked around and her eyes met his before she could mask her feelings.

'I—I wasn't running——' she began, 'I was giving myself a moment to phrase a suitable apology.' The honest words rushed out, surprising her as well as Carson whose eyes flickered. 'What I hinted about your son—I wouldn't stoop so low.' He was silent, eyes running over her sideswept hair and the off-shoulder taffeta gown that glowed topaz against her pale-honey skin. Fairlie felt as if he'd touched her.

'Apology accepted,' he said with an arrogant tilt of his dark head. The sprinkling of silver in his hair was enhanced by an angled spotlight. He looked distinguished, compelling—miles in front of mere handsome. 'But I think you were rather over-estimating your influence with him anyway.'

'You certainly do make apologies difficult, Carson,' she said tartly. 'You and your son don't enjoy the best of relationships—one doesn't have to be a psychiatrist to work that out. And it wouldn't take much to widen the rift to impossible proportions. Almost anyone could do it as you must know if you're half as shrewd in private as you are in business. However, I repeat— it will not be *me* who does so. Only sheer temper made me say something that only brings me down to your level of tactics and I'm sorry for it.'

She left him then noticing a certain pallor about his face that seemed to bespeak anger. It was strange that she had ever thought him lacking in emotion.

'Did you send Carson Tate an invitation?' she demanded of Pieter as soon as she got him alone.

'Why my fairest—as if I would when I know how much you—um—hate the man.' She looked sharply at him as he hesitated over the word. 'He came with my charming customer, Geraldine. Listed on her invitation as "and friend".'

'Oh.'

'Cheer up darling, you seem to have upset him as much as he has you, if that's any consolation.' He nodded at her startled glance. 'Yes, I remarked that passionate little meeting of yours a minute ago. What, I ask myself, do two people who are at war, so to speak, find to talk about that is so very absorbing?'

Fairlie looked away from those penetrating blue eyes. Pieter put up a hand and carefully smoothed back a wayward strand of blond hair.

'And what do you answer yourself, Pieter?' she said lightly.

'Do you know my sweet, I find my own questions amazingly difficult to answer at times.'

'Perhaps I'd better stay with you for a while,' she said and tucked her arm in his. 'You seem to be talking a lot to yourself and it's no good for you.'

His laugh bellowed and he patted her hand with a massive palm. But he looked again at Carson Tate and Fairlie thought there was perhaps some resentment in his eyes. Pieter was being protective again.

'Come, meet my southern colleague—he's rather interested in your work . . .'

In the end John Travis, who had a Sydney gallery, made a concrete offer to include her in a joint exhibition and Fairlie would have been delighted except that her recent move, the preparation of this current exhibition and her car had left her temporarily low on funds.

'Get a sponsor,' John Travis said as if it was the easiest thing in the world to find someone to pay her freight and insurance expenses and she knew from experience that it wasn't. 'If you can find a firm to back you, I'll be happy to feature their name in the gallery. Discreetly but prominently. Tell them there will be television and newspaper exposure and a monied, influential clientele . . .'

Fairlie was dubious but Pieter promised to talk to every monied acquaintance of a cultural persuasion. So there was a slim hope it might come off.

Geraldine Hallam was in some ways as Fairlie had pictured. She barely topped Carson's shoulder, her figure was slim and she was exquisitely dressed. But she neither wore the triple-row pearls nor the aristocratic disdain that Fairlie had concocted in a ridiculous moment of pique. Gerri, as she preferred to be called, was instantly likeable and wore about her the air of a woman who was rather lost. She also wore a wedding ring. Pieter informed her that Gerri's husband had walked out on her with his twenty year old secretary—a girl twelve years younger than Gerri.

'Up until then they seemed like a perfect couple.' Pieter sighed and spread his formidable hands. 'As I said before—strange things happen between men and women. Suitable people sometimes find they do not suit and sometimes—sometimes those who seem entirely unsuitable are made for each other.'

He looked over at Carson and Gerri and back to Fairlie.

'You think *they* are made for each other?' she asked reluctantly, eyes on Carson.

'No, my dear Fairlie, that is not that I meant at all,' Pieter said heavily. Then he snatched a bottle of wine from a waiter and insisted on pouring a drink to celebrate her further showing in Sydney.

'If I find a sponsor——'

'There is always Colossus. They back sports, I wonder if the arts would appeal to——'

'No!' She clutched the hollow stemmed goblet so hard that Pieter touched her pale knuckles and made a murmuring protest.

'It was a joke my sweet—where is your sense of humour?'

As she belatedly laughed, Fairlie felt that Pieter might have guessed where her sense of humour had gone. But it returned for two of her paintings sold that night.

Some days later Fairlie's crates arrived by rail at last from Melbourne and Nan lost no time in hanging her paintings in the house. These were pictures that her grandmother could enjoy to the full—Fairlie's favourites from her more traditional output. Landscapes and interiors with figures.

'Oh, Fairlie, isn't this one of——'

'Ben? Yes Nan.'

'You're *keeping* it dear?'

Fairlie smiled, her eyes on the painting. She had done it in her spare room at her flat. The room she had used as a studio. Her friend Janet was there, sitting astride a chair, her chin on her arms as she usually sat while she unburdened herself to Fairlie and behind her was Ben, leaning on the window ledge, one brow raised in his attractive, quizzical look. She had painted several portraits of Ben and only introduced him into this picture with Janet to provide an eyecatching vertical. Quite funny really. Yes, she was keeping this. To remind her of naïve, trusting days.

'Yes. Do you like it Nan?'

Nan liked it very much. Having seen her abstracts she was overjoyed to see that Fairlie had not completely abandoned painting 'normal' things. 'I'll hang it in the hall if it won't bother you having it around.'

So Ben hung in the hall. Suitable, Fairlie thought each day as she walked through and caught that quizzical gaze with a gradually lessening pang. Halls were for passing through. And Ben had only ever been passing through. After a few days she really felt the painting had stopped bothering her. Until she came home one afternoon and found Carson inspecting a landscape that Nan had hung just a few paces from Ben and Janet.

'I like your representational work,' he commented as he glanced over the outfit she'd worn that first day she'd met him. His gaze lingered on the tie.

'Thanks.'

As he began to move towards the other painting she forestalled him by coming closer. Suddenly she didn't want Carson looking at this picture with Ben in it. It was silly, illogical, but she knew as soon as he was gone that she would take it and hang it where he wouldn't see it.

'How is David?' she said, as a delaying tactic. Carson looked down at her, then at the picture. He almost seemed to sense that she didn't want him to see it.

'You'd know that better than I,' he said drily. 'I daresay he talks when he's here every afternoon.'

'Oh. Yes.' It had been a stupid question. She'd seen the boy only yesterday. 'You know I meant what I said Carson. Whatever our differences I wouldn't try to turn your son against you.'

He gave a short, dry laugh. 'That's already been done I'm afraid. But I believe you. I might have been rather ungracious about your apology last week.'

'You were.'

'Then it's my turn to say I'm sorry.' He took a step past her, closer to Ben's picture. 'Do you still paint both traditionally and abstract or are these earlier paintings?'

'Both—but more and more abstract now ... come into the lounge room. Nan has hung some better works there ...' She actually took his arm in her need to distract him. Carson captured her hand and looked at her.

'I'd like to see this one first.'

She made to disengage herself but he stepped forward and she was forced to go with him. So with her hand in Carson Tate's she looked again at the faces of the lover and the friend who had betrayed her. Her hand tensed under his and he moved his fingers to clasp her hand firmly. It was all unreal. Any minute now I'll wake, Fairlie thought, and find I'm not standing here holding hands with him. And liking it.

'Friends of yours?' he said looking at Janet and Ben.

'The girl had the flat next to me. And—the man ...'

At her pause he looked at her. 'So that's Ben?'

'Has Nan been talking?'

'She said you'd been engaged—that you broke it.' He looked again at the painting. 'It's a strong composition.'

'Isn't it?' Her laugh was wry. 'I should have put myself in the picture.'

'He strayed I take it?'

'That's one way of putting it.'

'You didn't give him a second chance?'

'That *was* his second chance.'

'Uh-huh.' Carson studied her, then turned back to Ben. 'He doesn't look right for you.'

'Oh my——' she woke from the dream, pulled her hand from his sharply, '——what a pity you weren't around last year. I could have shown you a picture of Ben and you could have saved me a whole lot of hassles.'

'If I'd been around then I might have seen you first.'

'Would that have been any advantage do you think?' she mocked and moved towards the kitchen door.

'We could find out. Have dinner with me tonight?'

Fairlie stopped. 'Why? Is Gerri busy?' She was sorry she mentioned the woman. Carson looked pleased that she had.

'Gerri and I are friends. But she is still crazy about her husband even though he left her.'

'Why ask me?' she said, annoyed to find pleasure from his disclosure about Gerri.

'I thought it was obvious. Because you're the first woman in years to take my mind off my work ... because you're interesting and outspoken ...'

'Interesting and outspoken,' she laughed. Her heartbeat picked up. 'Have you been reading a manual on non-sexist flattery?'

'——and because I fancy you,' he added in a low voice. Just the words played up and down her spine, reminded her of that night in his office when he'd kissed her and told her he wanted her. In this at least he too was outspoken. Her skin tingled.

'A good old-fashioned, chauvinist reason. I appreciate your frankness Carson, but no thanks.'

'Some other time then,' he said, unperturbed. 'When Nan and I have found a solution to our problem.'

'Nan and you—and *I*,' she corrected. 'Don't plan on leaving *me* out will you Carson?'

'I've no intention of leaving you out.' There was that underlying meaning there. She ignored it.

'Good.' As she reached the closed kitchen door, he took her wrist to delay her.

'Tell me—why didn't you want me to see your painting with Ben in it?'

'Oh—it embarrasses me I suppose. It's not awfully good. I should have made a better job of it.'

'Paint over it,' he suggested. 'And start again.'

'Is that advice from an art lover, Carson?'

'No. From someone else who made a poor job of it.'

'And have you started again?'

He opened the door into the kitchen. Mondo Rock was playing. The smell of oven-fresh date loaf floated on the warm air to them.

'I'm trying damned hard,' he said. And they went in to see Nan who turned down her radio and offered them buttered date loaf while she told Carson again how very attached she was to her own kitchen in her own old house—and how she just wished it had been built somewhere else where it wouldn't stand in his way. If Carson had time enough to wait Fairlie thought, Nan might move out simply because she liked him so. Of course, Carson seemed to return her liking. His ease with her grandmother was not feigned. Neither was his warm smile and his amusement at being treated alternately as a V.I.P. and a mere boy to be plied with tea and her award winning date loaf.

'This loaf recipe has won two first prizes at past Ekkas,' Fairlie told him.

'Ekkas?'

'Brisbane jargon for Exhibition. In other words, Royal Agricultural Show.'

'Two first prizes,' he repeated and finished off a slice—'Yes, yes I can believe that. But perhaps just one more slice to satisfy myself that it really *is* that good . . .'

Nan willingly cut him more cake and laughed with him as he probed for her other successes at the show.

Yes, Fairlie decided as she lay in bed that night. Carson really did like Nan. In fact, he seemed to enjoy the atmosphere of her house, which was really rather ironic. Was it a taste of a home life he didn't have? 'I'm trying damned hard.' She relaxed, even though one of her last conscious thoughts was to wonder how Carson expected to solve the problem of Nan and her house. The other was more complex and drifted her into sleep with the oddly secure remembrance of standing with her hand in Carson's looking at faces that suddenly seemed years in the past . . .

CHAPTER SEVEN

A FORTNIGHT later Nan was still in her house and apparently untroubled. Fairlie on the other hand had problems. Her car, parked in the street due to the impassable drive, was side-swiped one night, the side dented and one headlight shattered. Worse, the driver's door was buckled and refused to open. She drove to work in it, feeling like the survivor of a demolition derby and her manoeuvres in and out across the passenger seat did nothing for her disposition or her crisp clothes.

David was walking on what was left of the footpath when she parked outside that afternoon. His eyes lit up with a schoolboy's delighted horror at the state of the car.

'Wow! What hit you?'

'I've no idea. Someone miscalculated during the night I suppose and left no calling card,' she sighed. 'I didn't bother insuring it either.'

Fairlie knelt to inspect the base of the driver's door and David did the same.

'Sure it was an accident?' he asked.

'If it wasn't it was an expensive thrill for someone. Their vehicle must be in a mess too.'

'I mean the firm. Colossus,' David said. 'One of those movers could ram your car easily.'

Fairlie held his gaze steadily. 'Are you saying that your father might have arranged this David?'

He shrugged. 'He could have. Just another reason to make you move.'

Funny, Fairlie thought. This time she hadn't even thought of that. And seeing David so ready to believe the worst made her own previous behaviour seem rather childish.

'You know I would have assumed just that once,' Fairlie ran a finger over the sharp pleats in the metal where the duco flaked off, 'I've made quite a fool of myself in fact, assuming things.' She smiled, remembering her wild accusations that James was a gigolo. 'Besides I think your father has enough on his mind without organising last rites for my poor old car.'

'He's only got one thing on his mind. Money.'

'It's more than money that's putting circles under his eyes.'

David looked up quickly then, holding her gaze as he stood. His eyes slid away beyond her and his closing expression told Fairlie who she would find when she turned around.

The odd look in his eyes and the permanence of his pose as he leaned against the rear end of her car made her think that Carson had been there some little while—long enough to hear her championing him to his son.

'Bad luck,' he commiserated.

'Yes, isn't it?'

'Have you had a quote on repairs?'

'Yes and I'm beginning to think that panel beaters must all holiday at Club Med if the price I was given is at all typical.'

He smiled. 'Our men could have a look at it if you like. We have our own workshop and the job could be fitted in when they haven't much to do. It might take a little longer though.'

'No, I don't think so. But thanks.'

'Don't be hasty. Our men don't holiday at Club Med. Come to dinner with us tonight and talk about it. Mrs Strachan always cooks too much for us, doesn't she, David?'

The boy stood up from another inspection of the damage which seemed to fascinate him.

'Yes, she thinks I've got King Kong's appetite. Please come Fair—Miss Jones.' He darted a look at Carson. 'I'll show you the model plans I've been working on. It's going to be solar powered.'

They all began walking up the small slope to Nan's house and the Colossus building. Nan's lawn had a shaggy, spring look about it—it would need mowing soon ... dinner at Carson's home? Fairlie thought giddily.

'You know that doesn't look too difficult a job. Apart from the door,' David said.

'What do you mean?' his father asked.

'Me and my mate worked on his father's station wagon and it turned out pretty well. Of course you have to get the right tools.'

Carson chuckled. 'Miss Jones might think twice about letting you loose on her car. Of course I could give you a hand I suppose on weekends. That way it wouldn't cost her anything——' he looked sideways at Fairlie, '—or hardly anything.'

Fairlie stared. Was he kidding? With his workload—take on panel beating on the weekends? Her eyes went to David. Of course. If he could get close to his son he would do even that.

David was sorely tempted to pursue the subject she could see, but pride was holding him back. They reached the house and Carson said to her, 'I'll be leaving the office at around six. Will you be ready?'

'No—I don't think——' she began.

'Not nervous of me still, Fairlie?'

'Nervous is the wrong word.'

He smiled. 'Come. Please.'

The simple words had a powerful effect. 'All right, I will,' she said. 'Thank you.'

'Can I go in to see Mrs Holborn for a while?' David asked his father.

'You haven't been invited.'

'Aw, I've got a standing invitation, Dad.'

There was a moment's silence. It was the first time Fairlie had heard David say 'Dad' and watching the quickly veiled pleasure in the man's eyes, she wondered if it was the first in a long time for him too.

'Okay then,' he agreed in a too-crisp voice. 'But be back at the office at five to start your homework.'

He turned away, his tall figure erect as he took the path to the Colossus building. Fairlie couldn't think what there was about that confident, straight-backed man that moved her so. He looked the picture of one who needed no one. But it wasn't true. Maybe that was why she felt like this.

Nan was bright-eyed and surprised when Fairlie told her that she would be dining with the Tates.

'Well,' she said, face alight with curiosity, 'that will be nice won't it, David?'

David's answer, muffled as it was by a thick insulation of pikelets, jam and cream, was nevertheless unmistakably positive.

Nan sat at her crocheting and David leafed through a photograph album looking at pictures of the old house when it was young, a pretty young woman in a cloche hat and a tall, young man called James. Fairlie went to her room and tried another letter to her father. The seven years between made the words stiff. 'Dear Dad, It is so long since you left and maybe I didn't

understand why you had to go at the time . . .' She
wrote for several minutes and re-read it with a heavy
heart. It was so accusing. She tore off the sheet and
tossed it in the wastebin where all her other efforts had
gone.

At five o'clock, David went obediently to Colossus
to do his homework and Fairlie showered and dithered
a bit over what to wear. At last she settled on a pale
grey knitted skirt and top of such dire austerity that
Carson could not possibly suspect her of trying to
dazzle him, but which she knew quite well had the
reverse effect of her business clothes. As she buttoned
the clinging top and tied the belt about her waist, she
was aware of the excitement building up in her. With
her make up on and her hair flipping wildly about her
shoulders, she gave herself a wry smile in the mirror.
Dining at Carson's home. Next she would be getting
to like the man. Her tongue flicked over her lips. It
was an innocuous word. But 'like' had a spring-board
sound to it. From liking, it was so easy to dive off into
deeper waters. And she had proved to be a poor diver
in the past.

Carson and David collected her in the Rolls and
Nan waved away any suggestion that she might be
lonely. She fluttered a lace-edged handkerchief from
the verandah as they drove away. The vehicle made
its way along Coronation Drive and then to a leafy,
riverside street. Carson parked beneath an apartment
building and they took a lift to the penthouse suite.

Its view was as sweeping as that from his office—
only here it was the winding reaches of the river that
dominated and the dusking, dark shapes of spreading
trees with the thrust of palms here and there against a
dust-pink sky and silver-pink water. The furniture was
austere in design, lush in upholstering. Fairlie sank

into a chair while Carson disappeared briefly then came back to pour drinks. He handed her one and sat opposite her.

'Do you need any help with the dinner?' she asked.

'No. I can manage.'

'Oh? "Woman's place is in the kitchen"—wouldn't that be one of your slogans?'

'I'd be a brave man to fly that banner with you.' He grinned. 'No, it's not one of mine. Too limiting by far.'

Fairlie flushed and hoped that the rosy dusk light would account for it. When David came in with his plans for a solar powered mill she was glad of the distraction.

'I thought I'd build it in the spare room,' he glanced at his father and it was clearly a sulky request for permission.

'A mill in the spare room ...' Carson said thoughtfully, 'could be a problem with the ceiling. Of course we could knock a hole in it I suppose—build one of those perspex steeples over it to protect it while you're building ...'

They both stared at him.

'. . . and the grain could cause some ructions with Mrs Strachan. You know what she's like about her floors.'

'Grain?' David repeated. 'Perspex steeple? But it's not ...' He laughed. 'It's a model—less than a metre high, Dad.'

Carson mocked dawning comprehension. 'Ah, of course. A model. Much more appropriate for a penthouse. But,' he raised his brows regretfully, 'no crushed grain? We could buy a budgie or two to eat it.'

'You're having me on,' David said with a smile just

visible on his down-turned face.

'Afraid so. I always was a terrible tease.'

David spread his plans on the floor and crouched over them. 'Yeah, I'd forgotten,' he mumbled.

Fairlie sat down on the carpet and David explained his project to her. 'Trouble is, I'm not sure about the framework. I could weld it or I could use some pre-fab stuff that bolts . . .' Carson lowered himself to study the plans, saying nothing for a time.

'Did you draw these up yourself, David?'

'Of course,' the boy said defensively. 'But that doesn't mean I want to be an engineer.' 'Like you', the unspoken words sounded clear enough and Carson's jaw tensed. Fairlie willed him to let it pass and he did. As he casually went on to ask questions and offer a suggestion or two, she sat and watched them, amazed at the strength of her wish for harmony between them both. For the boy's sake. David looked up at Carson with guarded interest in something he was saying and the man's hands moved in explanation. For the man's sake.

Feelings came crowding in on her, muddled, undefined. But intense. She sat there, bombarded by a whole new sensation and when Carson looked at her it was as if he'd picked up her signals. As David rolled up his plans, Carson's eyes held hers across the small space and Fairlie had to turn away first.

'About your car,' Carson said after he had made a quick trip to the kitchen again. 'Would you like to let our workshop have a look at it?'

She hesitated.

'Go on, Miss Jones. If you put it in our workshop, I might be able to work on it too,' said David.

She looked at the boy thinking how easily that 'our' came to him now that he wanted something. Happy enough to be a Tate when the occasion suited. On Carson's behalf she was annoyed.

'You might need to check with your father about that, Sholto,' she said mildly and David coloured at this sidelong reminder of his eagerness to change his name.

'Sholto?' Carson questioned, eyeing his son's sheepish face.

'Just a pet name.' Fairlie shrugged. 'All right, I'll accept your offer Carson. Name me a reasonable price and I'll let David use it as a guinea pig provided he has your permission.'

The matter was settled. The car would be available for her during her work period and go to the workshop each afternoon. David would be allowed to help for a half hour each day and one weekend perhaps.

'Half an hour,' David complained. 'That's peanuts.'

'When you start at the bottom, labouring—the pay is peanuts too,' his father told him.

'Is that where you started Carson? At the bottom?'

'More or less. The Tate Corporation started as a family business—but I'm sure you know that story.' He smiled faintly. 'My father and his brothers had certain rules that sophistication didn't change. One was that the men at the top should know more than just where to sit at the boardroom table. I studied engineering and management and in the Uni holidays worked at whatever jobs were going in the firm. I've been a member of four unions.'

'Grandad said——' David began, then clammed up and shook his head when Carson prompted him. He took his plans and left the room. Minutes later the shower started, closely followed by a stereo blast of Duran Duran then the bathroom door closed, muffling the noise.

Carson's jaw tightened. 'David was staying with my parents when Tricia left on her honeymoon. I had to play the heavy to bring him up here with me. That's one of the reasons he won't talk to me.'

'Play the heavy? Surely as his father you have every right——'

'Tricia wouldn't give her permission for him to travel inter-state so I had to get a court order. But court order or not, when he doesn't want to come with me and my parents don't want to let him go, it makes for one hell of a fight.' And though he'd made a fight of it, David still thought Carson didn't really want him. What kind of a family were these Tates?

'Fight?' she said. 'Over a boy?'

'Mum and Dad don't approve of me. As a father that is. God knows I made a few mistakes as a husband and I'm not doing too well at parenting—but their opinion has been influenced by my ex-wife.' He half smiled. 'After the divorce she remained on excellent terms with them. Better than me, ironically.'

'But why would she sabotage——' she stopped, conscious that the question was a very big step inside Carson's territory.

'Tricia has never forgiven me.'

'Oh. I see,' she said, disappointed to have him confirm that he was another male betrayer.

'I don't think you do. It wasn't me who went outside our marriage, not in the conventional sense. My mistake was taking my work as my mistress. That left Tricia alone a lot. Until she tired of being alone. It was as much my fault as hers, I guess. But she didn't thank me for saying so. She has never forgiven me for forgiving *her*.' He put his head back and looked at her between half-mast lids. 'I daresay that sounds crazy to you.'

'A little. But I think I can understand that better than I can your parents being influenced by your wife, knowing that she'd had an affair ...'

'Ex-wife,' he corrected. 'And they don't know about Tricia's boyfriends.'

She noted the plural. 'Then why don't you tell them?'

His eyes went to the door through which David had left. A faint bass beat came from the bathroom. 'Because David might find out.'

He was quite a man. And he cared even more than she'd thought. Though his own image had been chipped away by Tricia—and by Greg, she suspected—Carson refused to cast aspersions on the boy's mother.

'David's an intelligent boy. Soon he'll evaluate the situation himself.'

'I'm counting on it,' he said.

Fairlie was silent for a few minutes. She had asked and the answers had carried her further forward than she had anticipated. She had walked out on to the edge of the springboard and below were deep waters.

'Does your father have any part in running Colossus?' she asked, trying to keep her balance.

'Not directly, thank God. But I have to report to the Tate board and my father and uncles expect me to come up with the kind of miracles they themselves performed. As the years pass I'm afraid their early exploits become more and more incredible. I'll never be the man my father was ...' He gave a wry smile.

'You don't believe that.'

'Oh yes I do,' he said fervently. 'They were all hell-raisers in some ways. But they've become legends almost and now they believe their own publicity machine. They forget that along with their successes they made some horrific blunders.' Her mouth twitched. It sounded very much as if Carson Tate was not always the boss. 'It's one reason I decided to set up the office in Brisbane myself,' he sighed. 'In Melbourne they were always breathing down my neck. Three legends—plus several cousins after my job. Thank God they've been too busy to come up here to check on me.'

'Not running scared are you, Carson?' she smiled.

'You haven't met my father and uncles. Or my most ambitious cousin,' he said drily.

'Are they like you?'

'There's a strong family similarity, yes.'

'And this cousin—is he like you too?'

'Tough as nails, ruthless, charming when necessary, highly intelligent and cunning.'

'He *is* like you.'

'She.'

'What?'

'My most ambitious cousin is a she. Wears suits and shirts and ties.' He grinned. 'Lorelei frightens the life out of me.'

She laughed at that. 'Lorelei?'

'Unusual but suitable. The Loreleis always were dangerous to men.'

Carson can't abide aggressive women, James had told her. And she had turned up in shirt and suit and tie with apparent nerves of steel. It explained a few things.

'In that case I'm not surprised you turned tail.'

'Turned tail? No such thing. A strategic retreat.' He picked up his drink and the diminished ice cubes rattled. 'Sometimes it pays to back off for a while.'

Was that what he was doing in the case of Nan—was that another strategic retreat? And perhaps it was what he was doing with her. 'I want you' he'd said and since then had done little in the way of pursuit. Carson smiled at her—a heavy-lidded, knowing smile—and collected her empty glass. She was warmed and warned by that smile. How long, she wondered, did his strategic retreats last?

They ate Mrs Strachan's lasagne and around nine David took his leave and went to his room to study. 'Thanks for coming, Fair—Miss Jones.'

'Make it first names if that's okay with Fairlie,' his father conceded. The boy said good night to her then paused.

'Good night, Dad,' he said.

The pleasure in Carson's eyes belied his offhand reply and after David had gone he looked so long at Fairlie that she thought he was going to remark on it. Instead he got up.

'Coffee, Fairlie?'

'Are you making it?'

'Of course. Yes or no.'

'Yes.'

'Ah,' he sighed mockingly. 'How I've waited for that "yes".'

'It's only coffee.'

'Haven't you heard of assent on a minor point? Having said yes once, even to something unimportant, it's easier to keep right on saying yes when the answers are vital.'

'If your next question has to do with Nan's house, the answer is no.'

His smile disappeared. 'You just can't bring yourself to trust me can you? All right, I admit I set up the office in Nan's house hoping to gain her confidence, change her mind. But——' he shrugged, '—instead I came to see how much the house means to her. I'm trying to solve the problem and so far haven't come up with anything much. But I won't do anything to harm Nan.' He waited there a moment. 'In any case, it's too early for my next question.'

With an odd smile he left her then. Fairlie went to the windows and looked out. All the warm pink and apricot of the sunset had been smudged out by indigo. Her whole body tingled at that next question.

Carson came back with a tray of coffee. He closed the drapes, making the large interior an intimate place contained within the light circle of two lamps. With a glance at her tense figure he went to switch on some music. Nothing romantic please, she implored silently. But something Wagnerian assaulted the speakers. He turned the volume down before sitting in an armchair. She hoped he wasn't reading all her mind so well, and poured the coffee, bending to the task so that her hair fell forward shielding her face from him.

'Just like Lorelei,' he murmured. Fairlie was rather dismayed at that.

'I'm not wearing a shirt and tie tonight.'

'But you're dangerous to men.'

She laughed. 'Will you turn tail again then, Carson?'

'No. Some danger I enjoy.'

She handed him a cup of coffee. 'Then enjoy this. But be careful. It's hot.'

'Familiar words,' he chuckled. 'If I burn myself will you administer first aid as I did to you?'

'Oh, I doubt it. I'm no thrill-seeker.'

His laugh shouted out. 'That *could* be flattery I suppose.' There was a wicked gleam in his eyes as he leaned forward to put his cup on the table. The London Philharmonic lashed out. 'Talking of thrill-seeking, had you ever driven an earthmover before that day?'

'Of course not. The most dangerous thing I'd ever driven before Old Ripper was my first car.'

'Why was that?'

'It was a bomb. I thought I was pretty smart and I went and bought it by myself. Just eighteen years old and a babe in the woods. I marched right into the clutches of a second-hand car dealer who couldn't believe his luck.'

'What was wrong with it?'

'Everything,' she said gloomily. He chuckled. 'My father couldn't believe it. He wanted to come with me to choose a car but I wanted to be independent—so I went without him.' And later, when it mattered more, he went without me.'

Her eyelids flickered. She raised her coffee cup and reluctantly answered when Carson asked about her father.

'He was a bit of a drifter with jobs. Always changing, trying something new. Somehow he never had any money, never owned a house—but my mother adored him. He had a lot of talent for art, more than I have, but never developed it properly. I think he was very frustrated in some ways . . .'

'Didn't Nan tell me he was living in Canada?'

'Yes. Why?'

'You talk as if he's dead.'

Fairlie gulped on hot coffee. No. No! She only used the past tense because her father had made it so. He had gone and left her, mistaking her proud bid for independence for the real thing.

'Just a turn of phrase,' she said. 'I haven't seen him since I was nineteen. After a gap that long you tend to think in the past tense.'

He nodded, made no comment. It seemed likely that he knew all about this from Nan. She wanted to be angry at that but anger wouldn't come. The Wagnerian music finished. Carson replaced it with something gentler. Fairlie leaned back into her chair. Opposite her, Carson relaxed, his big body graceful in repose. Eyes closed, his head tilted back against the chair and the line of his neck flowed strongly into the powerhouse chest. She followed the contour of his shoulders out and down along strong-made arms to his hands. He had attractive hands—large and square but sensitive. She remembered their touch . . . Carson opened his eyes as if he felt her regard.

'You'd make a good portrait subject,' she said, trying to sound more artist than woman.

'I'll pose for you.'

'You wouldn't like it. Hours and hours of doing nothing.'

'I'd be looking at you.'

'Would that be enough to keep you from boredom?'

'From boredom, yes. But come to think of it, looking at you wouldn't be enough. I'd want to touch.'

'In that case I won't paint you,' she said lightly. 'There's nothing worse than a fidgety model.'

He laughed. ' "Fidgety" implies a lack of concentration. I wouldn't be fidgety at all.'

His voice was heavy with promise. Fairlie's breathing quickened. Her body warmed as if he'd actually touched her. While she searched for something spell-breaking to say, Carson went on, 'Nan tells me you're hoping for a sponsor for your Sydney showing. Isn't that unusual?'

'Not unusual exactly. But hard to get. Pieter seems

to think he might find someone to pay my freight costs and insurance in return for some advertising.'

'Have you sold anything at the gallery?'

'Just two paintings. My work isn't everyone's cup of tea.'

'No,' he agreed and got up to put another record on. His flat honesty pleased her.

While he took a new record from its sleeve, she went to the window and pulled aside the drapes to look at the starlit sky and the light-sprinkled St Lucia scape. She was restless, her body alive with anticipation and she wanted to deny it. 'I think it's time that I——' she began and turned around to find Carson an arm's length away, '—went home,' she finished huskily as Ravel's *Bolero* settled into the compulsive rhythm of destiny.

'Fairlie,' he said and his voice was as husky as hers. He held out his hand to her.

'I really must be going——' she gulped. 'Nan might wait up and—and . . .'

It was too powerful for her. That outstretched hand. She put hers in it, felt his fingers close warmly on her. It was crazy. They were far apart yet she felt a warm intimacy as if he had her close in his arms. With no more than the touch of his hand to make it physical, she was making love with him, in her mind—knowing already as a woman the lines of his body she had admired as an artist.

'—and there's work tomorrow . . .' she whispered as he drew her to him. Even then he didn't hold her. She was free to do as she wanted. And she stayed. Carson touched her face, sliding his hand beneath the fall of her hair to stroke her cheekbone and jaw in a tender gesture. When it came, his kiss was a caress—a touch scarcely there but one that rippled through her body. And still there was space between them, yet strangely no space. Fairlie sighed as he pressed a kiss to her temple then pushed aside her hair and laid his lips in parted sensuousness against her neck. Her hands slipped around his sides and with a great outrush of breath Carson held her at last and brought her close against him. This time he kissed her deeply and she opened to him, giving him a response that was unconditional ... no doubts, no suspicions could halt this. It was inevitable she thought and moved with him in desire and delight. He stooped and picked her up, whirling her dizzily about before sitting in one of his high-backed chairs with her held close on his knee. In sheer indulgence, she ran her hand over his arm and shoulder, followed the pure masculine line of neck and chin to the silver-touched hair above his ear. His head bent to her breast and she felt the pressure of his mouth through her clothing. Then, with his hand curved to her, he let his head drop back against the chair and watched her through half-closed lids. When his breathing slowed, he lifted his other hand to stroke her hair. Leaning against him, Fairlie wished their passion could take its course, even as she relished this quieter, more controlled intimacy. With her fingertips she traced the stubborn line of his jaw down to his chin. When she touched his lips he parted them and drew one fingertip inside and wrapped his tongue around it before he released her. She gasped and met his heavy, wanting eyes with her own.

'How I want you,' he murmured and his hand played over her breast, finding the tip to tease it through her clothes.

'Then why not—of course, I forgot. David.' He smiled at her honesty. She wanted him too and wasn't bothering to hide it.

'Even if David wasn't here I wouldn't ask you to share my bed,' he told her. 'Because you don't trust me yet.'

'That has nothing to do with this, Carson.'

'At first I didn't think so either. But at first I just wanted to make love to you. It was a purely physical reaction to a lovely, challenging, man-hating woman.'

'And now?' she whispered.

'Now I—can't think of you in just those terms. I like you, dammit——' His hand clenched in her hair. 'Which complicates things my darling. I want your trust when you come to me.'

When you come to me. It had a strong sound. A permanent sound. Fairlie tried to hold in her elation. It was premature and founded on so little. But it wouldn't be held back entirely.

'I like you Carson—I didn't want to, but I do.' Like. That powerful word. If they were saying 'love' now it would mean nothing. But *like*. A fool again ... she told herself, but it felt so good. So right. For now.

Lazily he stroked the hair from her forehead. 'When did you find that out?'

'It just crept up on me. And you?'

'Same here. Pretty sneaky, hey?'

He held her there a moment as the music gained in power, drawing Ravel's ill-starred lovers to their fate.

'If we stay here,' Carson murmured, 'we might end up leaping into the volcano too.'

Fairlie resisted his gentle push. Her arms slid around his neck. 'Not nervous of me are you, Carson?' She used his words.

He groaned. 'Like you said, nervous is the wrong word. Get up Fairlie.'

She laughed—a little high, a little reckless with this crazy new feeling.

'Do I really take your mind off your work?' She breathed the words into his ear. 'You told me I was the first woman in years to——'

Carson grasped her wrists and pushed her upright, following closely. 'Yes you do. And you are. Now I'm taking you home you Jezebel.'

She picked up her bag while he went to check on David. When he came back the music was rising to its inexorable, passionate end. Carson silenced it.

'Just in time,' he murmured as he took her arm.

CHAPTER EIGHT

THE following day she ploughed into Sam Elliott's statistics using her calculator and only half her brain. The rest was occupied with Carson. There was no evading the issue, she thought as lunch and her knock off time approached. Last night she had slipped off the springboard of liking and was falling—falling. Fairlie knew it was probably the most foolish thing she'd ever done—getting involved with Carson. But the knowledge didn't dull the light in her eyes, the glow in her face that Nan had remarked over breakfast with a canny, 'My, you're looking radiant today dear.'

At twelve-thirty she tidied her desk and smiled vaguely at Sam Elliott as he came up to her, scratching his ear and looking a bit self-conscious.

'Just leaving, Fairlie? How about a favour? Bronwyn's going home early today. Could you give her a lift uptown to catch her bus?'

Such was her state of mind that Fairlie forgot all her resolutions concerning Bronwyn. 'Sure,' she said, and a few minutes later assisted the girl into the car's back seat. She herself slid in across the passenger seat because of the crumpled door.

'Having a half day off?' she said, trying to shed her preoccupation.

'Not exactly. I've been feeling a bit funny this morning and Mr Elliott told me to go home.'

Fairlie felt the first flutterings of uneasiness. 'Funny?' she repeated. 'How funny? Not every three minutes type funny I hope.'

'No. Only five,' Bronwyn said, cool as you please and Fairlie stood on the brakes before they got out of the car park.

'It's okay, first babies are hardly ever early. This is probably just another false alarm. If you could drop me off at a taxi rank ...' The girl clutched her stomach and bit her lip for a few seconds. 'Whew, that one was a bit fierce,' she said in surprise.

'I knew it—I knew it——' Fairlie muttered and thought of treacherous Sam Elliott passing the buck. 'I'll drive you to the hospital.'

But it wasn't that simple. In spite of her increasing discomfort Bronwyn insisted on collecting her bag from home where she left a message for the prospective father should he prove unavailable at the office, and Fairlie drove at a cracking pace with anxious glances at her passenger. Her face was looking decidedly shiny though she continued to suggest it was another false alarm.

'It's not due for another three weeks ...' she kept saying.

Then the car that had been around the country on Highway One, broke down. Fairlie took one look at Bronwyn and didn't bother opening the bonnet to spot the trouble. She took off her high heels and ran barefoot to the nearest 'phone to ring a cab. The driver looked resigned when he pulled up and a distressed Bronwyn got out of the battle-scarred sedan.

'Oh my gawd,' he said.

'Better you than me,' Fairlie retorted as they got in. 'But if you find a fast route to the Mater we might manage without the hot water.'

They did. The driver, giving instructions over the back seat to Bronwyn—'Yeah, that's right love—nice relaxed breathing just like you're doing—that's just lovely.' He used his horn to great effect and made the entry to the Mater Mothers in record time.

Then it was out of Fairlie's hands. All she had to do was wait until Colin picked up either of the messages left for him at the office or at home. She felt vaguely responsible. Someone should be here, she thought. Bronwyn's family all lived in Adelaide. She rang Nan to warn her that she would not be home for a while and told her about Bronwyn and the car which was stranded at Holland Park.

'Any news?' she kept asking the nursing staff and was amazed to find herself pacing about. So it really was true, she thought in a flash of humour—all those cartoons. An hour passed before Colin arrived gabbling nervously about Bronwyn getting her dates mixed. It was the only thing Fairlie heard him say that she understood—and agreed with.

It was a boy. 'A boy, a boy!' Colin yelled and almost hugged the doctor who made a quick exit. He hugged Fairlie instead. She looked over his shoulder and saw Carson standing in the corridor. It didn't seem odd at all just then that he should be there. She went to him, smiling. 'It's a boy,' she said foolishly and he put his hands to her waist and pulled her close.

'I'll take your word for it,' he grinned.

Colin came and shook Carson's hand. 'Sorry I haven't got any cigars,' he said, not even asking who he was. 'He arrived early.' Fairlie tried to explain everything to Carson but he apparently had a grasp on the matter for he produced a slim gold case of cigars from his suit pocket. Nan would have told him, Fairlie thought. Just why he had come though, caused her some puzzlement and an amazing warmth.

'Congratulations,' he said genially to Colin. 'I know the feeling.'

Fairlie stopped smiling, stopped stammering explanations and studied Carson as he drew on a cigar, trying to see him thirteen years ago—her own age—a delighted father of a newborn son. He had probably rushed, grinning and proud to his wife's bedside as Colin was about to do—held her hand and shared that supreme moment with the mother of his child ... she watched Carson's profile and jealousy stabbed at her. He had already had a lifetime—a woman had shared this with him and it would never be the same again for him.

Later, an arm about her, he walked her outside. 'Nan said you were here and that your car had broken down. Tell me where you left it and I'll arrange to have it towed to our workshop.'

'There's no need. I really can look after it myself.' She spoke more sharply than she intended, for the scenes of his other life were still there in her head—alienating her.

His jaw tensed. He closed the Rolls door on her with a snap. 'Beg pardon Ms Jones,' he said when he got in. 'My mistake. I thought you were liberated enough to accept some help.'

She sat silently as the car floated them through the city along the terrace above and then to Nan's road, past the house to the Colossus car park.

'Come up with me,' he clipped. 'I want to show you something.'

'No thanks. I have work to do.'

'So have I damn you.' Her arm was gripped hard and he towed her to the lift with little effort. 'If you want to make a scene go right ahead,' he said. 'My secretary won't turn a hair.'

'You drag women up here often do you?' she

retorted. 'She's used to you manhandling females is she?'

Carson propelled her into the lift, whirled her around to face him and crushed her in his arms in one powerful movement. His mouth came down on hers, hard and insistent and after a token resistance she relaxed and responded to the potent persuasion of his lips and tongue.

'I like you so much when you're silent,' he provoked, drawing away from her just as the lift doors slid open.

'You timed that nicely to coincide with the doors. Do you practise your love scenes a lot?' she enquired breathlessly.

'No. It's all pure instinct. Afternoon, Sandra,' Carson tacked on as they passed his secretary's desk.

Inside his office he nudged her to the architect's model of the project. 'Take a look.'

'I've already seen it,' she said. But there was a change. Some of the car park and landscaping were gone. A tiny house—Nan's house—perched in its proper place. Sprawled around it on three sides was Colossus Court.

'That's why the surveyors were around again. I've been re-looking at the situation for a while.'

'You can't be serious.'

Ruefully he smiled. 'I can't see any other way. Nan wants to stay in her house and we are committed to the project. Without her land we are restricted to two accesses into the parking area which means we can't comply with council standards so the architects have modified the building.' He pointed out the changes in design.

'But it looks—odd.' Could she believe this? Carson Tate of the battling, rip-roaring, takeover Tates, prepared to go *around* an obstacle, not over it?

'It's not what I want, I can't pretend otherwise. There is one other possibility but I don't think it will be feasible. The house may be too old,' he said cryptically and tilted his head at the scale model. 'So we're stuck with it. The finance company director is against it and the seniors will be mad as hornets when they find out but I think I can handle them.'

He stepped close behind her to take her shoulders. She felt the brush of his lips on her neck.

'So you see, you can relax Fairlie. Nan is safe. But I think I should warn you that you aren't . . .'

His arms folded about her midriff pulling her back against him. She closed her eyes as he pressed his mouth again to her neck. 'What are you doing tonight?' he murmured and put one hand to her breast, encompassed it warmly and with a stillness that seemed to indicate ownership to Fairlie.

'I'm going to visit Bronwyn and her baby,' she said, contrarily wanting to make it difficult for him.

'Ah, of course.' She expected him to argue but he simply looked down at her with a smile and said, 'Pity.'

Pieter was waiting when she got back to Nan's house. He was resplendent in an Indian collared cream shirt and a chain complete with a diamond studded pendant.

'Really Pieter,' she teased. 'Wearing your diamonds in the daytime.'

'Vulgar isn't it, my pet?' He hefted his bulk from Nan's groaning settee and held her delicately to kiss her forehead. 'I come with good news. You have a sponsor, Fairlie. K. M. Murchison & Co., makers of drainage pipes.' He pulled a face. 'Still, one can't have everything.'

'That's marvellous, Pieter. But Murchison? I've never heard of them.'

'My dear, why should you? But let us be thankful that their board has a sudden thirst for culture and, of course, a little discreet advertising with tax relief. John Travis is delighted and wants you down there for the opening week.'

'Down there? In Sydney?'

'Darling, didn't he mention it? I'm almost sure he did. He wants you to make a few appearances at the gallery in the initial promotion—draped in something green to match your eyes and ready to discuss in painful detail every little nuance your prospective buyers see in your work. The travel and accommodation costs will be covered by your sponsors.'

Fairlie was frankly amazed. 'Heavens, that's generous.'

'Drainage pipes are in big demand. Murchisons have the biggest market share in the sewerage department.' He repressed a shudder. 'I had it from the G.M. himself. You know, there is something wonderfully *modern* about sewerage pipe profits finding their way into art.'

Fairlie frowned. She had some small reputation in Melbourne it was true, as a promising contemporary artist, but sponsors, especially generous ones were scarce and she had landed one so easily. She said as much to Pieter, who waved a large hand and took full credit. 'I merely dropped a few words in the right ears and in a roundabout fashion they came to those of the Murchison G.M. If you must thank me my sweet, don't get lipstick on my shirt will you——' He gave her a piercing look. 'An unnecessary caution. Your lipstick appears to have worn off elsewhere.'

Fairlie crimsoned and kissed him on the cheek.

'Thank you Pieter. But I don't know if I can go to Sydney—my job you see. I wonder if Mr Elliott will let me go—oh, darn it I'll ask him. After all he owes me something for palming Bronwyn off on me when he must have known she was about to go into labour—it was a boy, by the way.'

'Of course.' Pieter led her to the couch and they sat down. 'Dare I say it is a little hard to follow? Tell me all about Bronwyn and her newborn . . .'

He chuckled with her as she related the afternoon's events, his big laugh billowing up from his bulk and vibrating the settee.

'. . . and then Carson arrived.' She stopped suddenly, her face colouring faintly.

'Something tells me that you and Carson are more friendly.'

'I don't trust him.'

'Pieter got up heavily. 'One should exclude the other but I gather it is not so?' he said with a stronger dose of accent.

'Do you think I should trust him, Pieter?'

His blue eyes flicked away. 'You ask me to recommend him to you, my dear?' Pensively he looked back at her. 'I wish I could say otherwise, but yes—I think he is a man you could trust.'

'What do you mean—you wish you could tell me otherwise?'

He ran a hand over his thinning hair.

'Because he is too good looking, has too much hair and is much, much too thin,' he said in mock asperity.

Fairlie laughed. 'Not jealous, Pieter? You know there is nobody like you. I wouldn't even dream of comparing Carson to you.'

He muttered something in Dutch, then went on in English. 'I know that my sweet. I know.'

When he had gone Fairlie realised that if she went to Sydney, Nan would be left alone for a week. It hadn't occurred to her until now that her absence might be to Carson's advantage. Her trust in him had taken a leap forward. Maybe too far. For that tiny house model on the Collossus Court layout had moved when she touched it. In the grounds of the scale model at least, Nan's house was by no means a permanent fixture.

'A boy! Oh, that's lovely.' Nan sighed when she heard about Bronwyn's safe delivery and hurried away to see if she had any three ply left to knit some bootees.

'But you don't even know Bronwyn,' Fairlie pointed out.

'As if that matters.' Within a half hour her knitting needles were clicking. 'What time will you visit her tonight?' she asked after a few rows and nodded complacently when Fairlie told her.

'You won't have them finished by then, surely, Nan?'

Her grandmother just smiled and knitted away, only stopping to greet and feed David when he arrived and dropped his school bag in the kitchen.

'I'm late,' he said. 'I had cricket practice today.' He chatted over a repast of jam tarts while Nan knitted, but when Fairlie went out he followed her.

'Fairlie—are you and Dad—I mean, are you his girlfriend now?'

'David—I don't really—all I know is that I started off disliking your father and now I like him. I like him a lot.'

David fiddled with the pocket of his trousers. 'You must have felt stupid finding out you liked him after all the awful things you said to him.'

She saw what he was getting at. His young face was stiff.

'Oh—pride you mean. It's very overrated.' On

impulse she hugged him. He pulled away with an offended male look. 'Sorry,' she laughed. 'Just be glad of Nan's jam tarts.' He looked puzzled. 'They're all over your face—otherwise I might have kissed you as well.'

He rubbed the back of his hand over his mouth and grinned. 'I think I'll go and have another one.'

Fairlie went to her room.

'Dear Dad,' she wrote, 'I can't pretend I'm not resentful because I am. Even now I wish that I had been reason enough for you to stay . . .' She ripped the page off and crushed it, thinking of Colin's face at the hospital today. Her own father must have looked like that the day she was born—and Carson, at David's birth . . . her thoughts circled, merged and she closed the writing folder.

Nan had one bootee finished and threaded with ribbon left over from the half dozen pairs she'd made for cousin Cecil's latest baby. Carson arrived to collect David. He smiled warmly at Fairlie then picked up the tiny, beribboned garment.

'I remember tying some like this on to you when you were a few days old, David. It gave me the fright of my life when I saw your legs.'

David was semi-sulking again, but couldn't let that pass.

'Why?'

'Oh, I suppose I had football boots and tennis shoes in mind for my son and when I lifted up your nightie——'

'Nightie!' David said, disgusted.

'Nightie. Under it were two of the skinniest, scrawniest little legs I've ever seen. No thicker than my finger.' He held up his hand. 'I tied those bootee things on to *real* carefully in case I squashed you.'

'You're having me on again, Dad.'

'You think so? Have a look at this then.' He felt for a leather folder inside his jacket. Two photos were revealed when he let it drop open. One of a close-fisted baby in napkin, skinny legs bent and mouth wide open in a howl. The other showed David at about ten, wearing an ASPRO cardboard hat and clutching a Dagwood dog and several sample bags. Beside him was Carson with his arm about the boy's shoulder.

'I remember that—you took me to the show. That was the last time . . .' He fell silent as Carson replaced the folder in his pocket.

'Do you always carry that around with you?' David asked without looking up. Carson glanced at Nan and Fairlie. His cheeks were tinged with unusual colour.

'Yes,' he said. 'I always carry it.'

In the end they all went to the hospital—a plan devised jointly by Nan and Carson and fruitless objections by Fairlie. She was swept along and her sense of humour came to her rescue just when she was despairing of keeping some sort of thinking distance between herself and Carson. He acquired a huge bunch of flowers at the hospital florist and even Bronwyn's cheerful placidity was overturned by the arrival of three complete strangers—a pink cheeked old lady proffering tissue wrapped bootees, a uniformed schoolboy and Carson dominating the room with his height and gladioli. They all trooped along to the viewing window and admired the baby which bellowed throughout, its tiny fists quivering on long, skinny arms. Colin pointed out his resemblance to various members of his family which was a waste of time as none of them knew them or were likely to, and Carson pointed to the tiny, bandy legs.

'Just like that you were,' he said in an undertone to David.

'Oh, gave me a break, Dad. He's ugly,' he said and Nan shushed him.

'You'll upset the baby's parents. Parents always think their babies are beautiful,' she assured him.

It should have been completely boring she supposed, but Fairlie looked around their odd little group and realised that they were all, including herself, enjoying it. Bronwyn sat like a queen, her hand in Colin's, saying little but glowing with achievement and Fairlie felt that pang of envy again. Across the welter of flowers, candies and baby rattles, she met Carson's eyes and she had the wierd sensation that she had almost completed that dive from the springboard. He looked relaxed, young and vital. His energy reached out to her through all those people and it was as if he'd touched her.

But he didn't touch her—not physically, that night. They went back to Nan's house and sat around the kitchen table for tea and boiled fruit cake and easy conversation.

'Your car is in a garage now I take it?' Carson said as they were leaving. Fairlie clapped a hand to her head. The car was still on the side of the road in Holland Park.

'I forgot about it,' she groaned.

Carson smiled. 'And you so capable. You don't seem to have progressed very far from that first car of yours.' It was a double barrelled comment. She'd bought a bomb and refused help then too.

Two more of her paintings sold and Sam Elliott agreed to make do with a temporary girl while Fairlie went to Sydney. He was somewhat sheepish as she had

known he would be about the breakdown of her car
and for dumping Bronwyn on her and she pressed her
advantage. The car was duly towed to a garage and the
repairs completed for an astronomical fee. Fairlie
almost regretted the surge of independence that had
prevented Carson from attending to it. But though the
car was functioning again, the chassis was still a mess.

On Friday, David called on his way home from
school as usual but with a friend this time. Alex, he
introduced him to Fairlie who was immersed in a
painting on the verandah. Rather absently she smiled
at the boys and only partly registered David telling her
that Alex's brother raced stock cars and that Alex's
hobby was working on car repairs.

'Oh yes?' she said, unable to pull her mind from her
developing work and she remembered saying 'yes' a
couple more times before the two uniformed boys
went inside.

She was still painting when Carson appeared. He
said nothing, just went quickly around behind her and
watched. Fairlie felt the pull of him there and after
maybe five minutes stopped work.

'Hello' She smiled and her eyes were soft in the few
unguarded moments between the kind of self-
hypnotism in which she worked and the awakening.
Carson came close and dropped a kiss on her mouth.
It was delicious—affectionate. She put a hand on his
shoulder and kissed him back. There was nothing
sexual about it—but as they drew apart Fairlie felt a
glow of pleasure, a serenity that tilted her mouth in a
dreamy smile.

'Why didn't I think of this sooner? I've been seeing
you at all the wrong times. In future I'll catch you
when you're working.'

She woke properly then, wiped the adolescent

dreaminess from her face. 'That wouldn't always be a good idea. When things aren't going right I swear and hate myself and everyone else.'

'I'd be prepared to risk it for a reception like the one I just had.'

'Well—you've been warned,' she said lightly and turned away to wipe her brushes.

'I hear you've given permission for David *and* his friend to work on your car. That was kind—and brave of you.'

'I what——? David and Alex?' She swung around, remembering all those yesses. 'I suppose I must have. They asked me questions and I was so absorbed I must have said yes once too often.'

Carson laughed. 'I did warn you about assent on a minor point. In future I'll *definitely* catch you when you're working.'

She shrugged. 'It doesn't matter I suppose whether it's one schoolboy or two. What harm could they do to a car that has already been around the country on Highway One?'

'True.' He nodded and stared at her painting while she capped her paints and swished the brushes in turps. She hoped he wouldn't say anything banal about it just to please her.

'What do you think?' she asked, curious to know what he *would* say.

'I think it is—strong, stubborn and aggressive.' He looked at her. 'And I like it. Very much.'

Carson smiled at her grimace and asked about her Sydney showing. He hadn't seemed very surprised when he'd found out that she would be exhibiting after all. It was a compliment of a kind, she supposed.

'Don't you want to know who my sponsor is?' Funny he hadn't asked.

He grinned. 'Let me see—B.H.P.? I.B.M.? The Bond Corporation?'

'No one so grand. K. M. Murchison. Drainage pipes. You've probably heard of them in your business.'

He nodded. 'I've heard of them. Where will you stay in Sydney?'

'The Sheraton-Wentworth. Drainage pipes are booming.'

'I'll miss you,' he said and went on to ask if the boys could work on her car over the weekend. He would catch up on some work in his office between trips to the basement workshop to supervise David and Alex, he said. She agreed.

On the weekend Nan's house was like a roadside café. David and Alex arrived at regular intervals to wash off grease and consume sufficient food to boost their energy and Carson, contrary to his talk of catching up on work, was rarely away from the house. In a T-shirt and faded jeans he looked like a big, energetic castaway as he roamed about doing odd jobs for Nan.

'I thought you had office work to do,' Fairlie said to him as he spent a great deal of time oiling the hinges on her bedroom door.

'Some things are more important. This weekend I'm ingratiating myself.' He took a good, long look around her room then at her T-shirted, shorts-clad figure.

'No need. Nan already thinks you're wonderful.' Fairlie rummaged in her dressing table drawer for her sunglasses.

'I'm not trying to ingratiate myself with Nan,' he said and she saw him watching her in the mirror. 'So how am I doing?'

You're doing just fine, she felt like saying. You're doing just great. I want to run to you and kiss you and tell you that I ... 'It's too soon to answer that question,' she said and put the dark glasses on. As she reached the doorway she looked up at him and added, 'You've only oiled a few hinges after all.'

'Ungrateful.'

She went downstairs and dragged Pa's old motor mower from beneath the house. The weather was glorious—Queensland's spring at its bluest, golden best. The frangipani was sprouting new leaves from its cushiony stumps and a few of the freesias that had been coming up for years were blooming in the tall grass near the parsley patch. On the clothes line, Nan's net kitchen curtains flapped in the breeze. That breeze and the sun had made Nan declare this 'a good drying day'. An accolade from an expert. Fairlie had only mown one length of the garden when Carson appeared coming purposefully towards her. She had half expected it. She didn't mind mowing grass. On a day like today she positively enjoyed it. She was fit and healthy and could do the job perfectly well. But a man just couldn't let this intrusion on to male territory pass.

Carson removed her from the mower simply by lifting her clear off the ground. The mower roared. So did she.

'Chauvinist!'

'Independent!' he yelled back and stripped off his T-shirt to toss it at her. He made a formidable sight. Big but gracefully muscled, none of the exaggerated bulges of the body builder. He bent and fiddled with the throttle of the mower and Fairlie watched the power play of his back and shoulder muscles in a kind of hunger. She touched her tongue to her lips and he grinned as he saw it. Looking over her bare legs again, he shouted, 'You look nice too, darling.'

So he thought she was impressed with all that male muscle did he, she thought as she ran up the back steps. If she had, for a moment, wanted to touch him it was nothing more than curiosity—the same as wishing to touch a sculpture—an artistic appreciation you might say.

'Something the matter dear?' Nan asked her and Faitlie found she had come to a halt in the kitchen. She was holding Carson's T-shirt high in one hand, her nose and chin buried in its Carson-scented folds.

'Nothing, Nan,' she flung the shirt over the back of a chair and went out wondering if she had dreamed all those adult years to age twenty-five.

CHAPTER NINE

SHE left for Sydney with an almost casual farewell
from Carson. But he added again, 'I'll miss you.'

The southern spring held a leftover winter chill.
Sydney was overcast. A few leaves rusting gold clung
still to the street trees near John Travis' gallery at
Woollahra and the wind whistled through the city's
canyons. There was wine and cheese and new money
and old at John's soirée style opening. Fairlie smiled
and obligingly talked to the sophisiticated clientele and
on the whole felt extraordinarily guilty that she had
been lucky enough to score a sponsor like Murchisons.
The other exhibitors were less fortunate as they took
pains to point out to her. She 'phoned Nan the first
evening and her grandmother seemed excited about
something. She had decided to spend the rest of the
week with the Reynolds, she told Fairlie. Her old
friends had been pressing her to visit ever since they
moved to their home unit. 'They haven't got the
'phone yet, so I probably won't speak to you until you
get back, dear.'

Fairlie was uneasy about it. She had a mental
picture of the old house on its stilts, empty—
surrounded by big, orange machines.

'You've got my hotel number, Nan, if you should
need me . . .'

It bothered her. Until the second night when
Carson 'phoned. His deep, smiling voice was reassur-
ing. Yes, he had seen Nan before she went to stay with
the Reynolds. And the house? He paused a moment at

the question and she regretted asking it. 'The house is just fine, Fairlie,' he said. 'And so is Nan. Your friend Bronwyn is going to get something knitted in "feather and fan", whatever that is.'

She laughed, relaxing. 'It's a speciality of Nan's, like her date loaf.'

'She sends her love.'

'You told her you were 'phoning me?'

'Every night.'

'You didn't ring last night.'

'Every night but last night. Don't split hairs.'

'Sorry,' she laughed and lay back on the bed pillows, cradling the receiver against her cheek.

'What are you wearing, Fairlie?'

The question startled her. Stretched out on the hotel's king sized bed, she drew the edges of her satin robe together.

'Why do you want to know?'

'I just wanted to picture you while I'm working.'

'Won't that be distracting?'

'I shouldn't think so,' he challenged. 'If it's that Prince Charming outfit of yours.'

'I'm wearing a cream satin robe and I'm lying on the bed . . .' She let the robe's edges fall apart again. There was a silence, then a wry chuckle.

'I *would* ask, wouldn't I? And I've got paperwork here piled as high as the Harbour Bridge. Do you miss me?'

'Miss you?' she echoed scornfully. 'Miss you tearing into Nan's cooking like a schoolboy? Miss your sarcastic double meanings and your oversized shoes clumping in the hall?'

'You miss me,' he said, all complacence. 'But chin up. I might have a surprise for you when you get back.'

Her heart began to gallop. 'Don't tell me. David has

built a four metre mill in your spare room—between
you you've wrecked my car chassis——'

He laughed. 'Nothing like that . . .'

The next day passed like the others. She was free
until eleven when the gallery opened and she
wandered about the harbour's edges, taking ferries and
perching on piers with her sketch pad and charcoal. A
surprise for her . . . she kept thinking, wishing the day
away so that she could hear Carson's voice on the
'phone again. But she didn't have to wait that long.
For that afternoon, when mild sunlight gilded the bare
trees outside John's gallery, Carson walked in.

Her smile was dazzling as she excused herself from
one of John's clients and went to Carson. He took both
her hands and looked down into her glowing face with
unsmiling intensity. His face still had all the wrong
angles. His mouth was as undistinguished—the lines
each side too deep. How fantastic he looks, she
thought.

'How soon can you get away?' he growled.

'Half an hour.'

'I'll wait.'

Just that. He turned away then and began to look at
the paintings. No reason for being here, no indication
as to what they would do when she was free. And she
didn't care.

John brought a silver-rinsed client over to be
introduced and she managed a conversation about her
work. Afterwards she couldn't remember what she
said for her eyes kept following Carson. In her mind
the doors of the gallery were already shut—in her
mind she was already with him. At last it was true and
Carson wordlessly guided Fairlie outside. He opened
the door of a car parked under the bronzed leaves of
an ash tree that leaned out over the iron railings of a

courtyard. As they drove away, fallen leaves scattered from the car's hood and flattened against the windscreen. Fairlie watched a leaf until it was borne relentlessly away by the wind. She didn't ask where he was taking her and Carson didn't say.

The car turned into the gates of Centennial Park and slowed along the roadway that ran parallel with the walking and bridle paths. They passed joggers and bicycle riders and two horsemen. Ducks on a pond. And waterhen. At length Carson pulled over beneath the scattered late afternoon shade of a Port Jackson fig. He got out and opened her door, took her hand and she ran alongside him as he strode down a slope to a grove of cypress.

'Just a minute,' Fairlie panted and bent down to remove her high heeled shoes. With them dangling from her hand she went with him, her feet sinking into the grass, until they reached the seclusion of the grove's low canopy. Then he tugged on her hand and turned to receive her into his arms.

'I thought I'd never get you alone,' he said and kissed her hard, crushing her against him and moving his mouth on hers in a hunger he didn't trouble to disguise. And his fire was hers. She had been ready for this for days, weeks—and she stood on her toes in the cold, shaded grass and threw her arms about his neck, her shoes still clutched in one hand. Close, through the trees, came the sound of children and the honk of a duck but they were sounds from another world. There was only Carson and the way he felt, the scent of him, the power and the need in him ... the delicious, tantalising touch of his mouth as their kiss tapered away to admit again the sweet sounds of the trees moving above, the cries of waterhen and gull.

'Carson, I'm so glad you're here,' she whispered foolishly into his jacket collar.

'I couldn't stay away.' He buried his face in her hair. She nestled closer and he flinched. 'Ouch!' Her shoe heels were pressed against his neck. 'Better put them on again. I wouldn't like to have to explain to anyone how I came to have stiletto prints on my neck.'

She put them on, then—arms around each other—they meandered through the trees to the pond.

'The park closes at sunset,' she said idly. 'It was on a notice near the gate.'

'We'll have to move on then. This was the only near place I could remember—I needed somewhere private to hold you and make me sane again.' And he steered her behind the bulk of a tree and tended again to his sanity.

The sun sent its last warmth rippling across the ponds and the park rangers clopped on horseback along the bridle paths. Carson took her back to the hire car and they drove at leisure out to The Gap where the open sea foamed against perpendicular rocks, then they went back along the inner side of the harbour's South Head past the gentler waters of the bays to the city.

They ate in a tiny Italian café which boasted stiff white tablecloths, huge bowls of pasta and a cellar, Carson declared, equal to any. The red wine might have intoxicated her had she not already tasted something headier. When they left arm in arm, Fairlie knew that her head had never been clearer, her heart never so sure.

'How long can you stay?'

'I'm flying back in about two hours which gives me time for a drink with you at the hotel before I drive to Mascot.'

'You came just for a few hours?' she marvelled.

'I had to see you. Strategic retreats are all very well but when *you* went away . . .'

The bars at the Sheraton-Wentworth were busy. Carson looked at Fairlie. 'They have room service here?'

'Yes,' she said.

In the elevator they stood apart watching with deep concentration as the floor numbers lit up. In her room, Carson went to the 'phone and ordered champagne. He stuck his hands in his pockets then, and went to the window to peer upwards.

'The weather has changed,' he remarked. 'No moon or stars tonight.'

The weather, Fairlie thought. Carson was feeling tension too.

'How is David?' she asked in her own bid for normality.

'Fine. He's staying at Alex's house tonight.' He paused. 'It's two steps forward and one back with David I'm afraid, but I think we've made some progress.'

He turned to answer the door, reaching for his wallet as he went. A few minutes later as he poured the ice cold wine, Fairlie said, 'Of course he resents the fact that you didn't remember his birthdays.'

His eyes flicked up at her, as they'd done that very first time, only now they were surprised.

'But you did remember, didn't you?' She took a glass from him.

'Yes.' He sighed. 'Tricia was very clever at denying me access—in the most civilised way, of course. I can see now I was a fool to stop insisting when she said my visits were upsetting David—give it time, she said. But to hold back the things I sent—and my letters too I suppose——'

'David didn't mention any letters. I did tell him at the time I thought it a bit odd about his birthdays. I pointed out that the very least a busy man like yourself would do would be to hand the job to his secretary.'

He smiled over his glass at her. 'Planting doubt? When was that?'

'Over the washing up the night you came to dinner with your "friend".'

'So long ago. I didn't think you were on my side then, Fairlie.'

'Not in anything else. But where David was concerned it was different. It was seeing you with your son that really made me think twice about you . . .'

'Oh?' His grey eyes were gleaming in the lamp light's soft glow. 'Not that rather pleasant interlude on my office terrace?'

Fairlie looked into her champagne, watched its fizz and recalled the impact of that first kiss.

'That made me think twice about myself rather than you. I was attracted to you but until I saw you with David I didn't really like you—wasn't even sure you had any deep feelings——'

The gleam in his eyes intensified. He put down his glass. 'But you know now. Do you trust me Fairlie?' He stood up and she tilted her head to meet his gaze. He came over and leaned forward, putting his hands on the arms of the chair so that his face was inches from hers. 'When you come to me——' he'd said.

'Yes,' she whispered.

The taste of champagne was on her lips and his when he kissed her. His mouth touched and drew away, his breath fanning her skin before his lips returned to hers, each time staying a fraction longer, each time asking a little more until he hauled her to her feet and into clamouring contact with him and shaped his mouth to hers in slow burning passion. Her arms went about his shoulders and she was vaguely aware that she was still holding her half empty glass. The thought was irrelevant and she dismissed it, dreaming, drowning in Carson's arms.

'Aagh!' he exclaimed and straightened. One shoulder and part of his shirt were soaked. The champagne had spilt.

'Is this a hint—an expensive substitute for throwing cold water on desire? First it's stiletto heels and now——' he began, plucking the wet material away from his skin.

Fairlie giggled. 'It's the classic situation. Now I'm supposed to say—you'll have to get that off or you'll catch your death of cold.' She set her glass down and unfastened his top button, unknotted his tie. 'Let me do it. I owe you *this* favour, don't I?'

She laughed again, remembering her own blouse tea-stained and Carson unbuttoning it without a trace of the tremor she was displaying now. Then his shirt hung open, his tie slithered to the floor and her hands slid over the broad contours of his chest. And Fairlie wasn't laughing anymore. With deep concentration she pushed away his damp shirt, smoothing it from one muscled shoulder then the other. In the lamplight his skin gleamed deep gold, a glowing contrast to the black hair that curled on his chest. Slowly, experimentally, she traced all the beautiful, masculine lines of his torso that she had admired and wished so much to touch that day in the garden.

'Not like touching a statue at all,' she whispered. No stone, no marble could have such duality—such silken softness over sheer strength. She smiled, remembering that she had excused her desire to touch him that day as mere artistic appreciation of form. What sculpture could offer so much?

'You're a beautiful man,' she said as he spread his hands to her hips and pulled her close to him.

His laugh was dry, husky. 'Is that the artist speaking, or the woman?' His dark head bent and he left the question mark against her lips. Their breath mingled.

'Both——' she sighed as he found the zip of her top and drew it slowly down. His fingers trailed over the bared skin of her back making her shiver with pleasure. He stepped back and lifted the garment over her head. And she was in his arms again, her skin registering the heat of his. Carson unhooked her bra, pushed it aside to explore her back and shoulders, then coaxed the straps down over her arms. Fairlie made a low sound of excitement as he curved his hands to her rib cage and pushed up, up until his thumbs were cushioned in the full lower swell of her breasts. Her nipples tautened, lengthened at the promise of that touch. Slowly he caressed her, folded her full flesh in his palms until she burned with wanting him. Legs planted apart, he lifted her feet clear of the floor and took the tip of a breast in his mouth, pulled strongly on it, wrapped his tongue about the nipple in small hungry caresses.

'Carson——' she gasped as the sensations multiplied. I love you, she said silently, her mouth moving against his shoulder where the skin tasted of champagne.

He put her down abruptly. 'Not like this. Not in a rush with a plane to catch.'

Plane? she thought, wondering at such irrelevance. Plane? She couldn't let him go. Not now. Her lips rested against his cheek. A faint roughness there.

Funny, she mused, wrapping her arms close about his beautiful, broad back. Deep water was only frightening from up on the springboard. Down here it was everything she'd ever dreamed.

'Then don't catch it,' she said. 'Stay.'

'You're sure?'

'I'm sure,' she whispered.

She went with him to the bed. Carson sat on the edge and put his arms about her to release her skirt. It fell to the floor and she stepped out of it. He removed her underwear with tender, unhurried hands and she was naked before him, looking down on his dark head as he kissed the newly bared skin. Her fingers closed in his hair—he touched and tantalised until he drew her on to the bed with him and tossed off the remainder of his clothes. She held his powerful body against her, then with a thrust within her. And there was tumult and his name and hers in husky, urgent voices as they moved together ... release ... and afterwards the languour, a quiet clasp of arms and tender touch of lips.

In the smiling light of the single lamp, Fairlie put a hand to his face.

'I thought you said there were no stars,' she said softly.

He touched his mouth to her forehead. 'I love you Fairlie.'

'Carson——' her hand stroked his rumpled hair '—darling Carson. I love you too.'

Fairlie's feet hardly touched earth in the days that followed. Sydney with its solid rock and mighty towers was unreality. She wanted to fly back, to be with Carson and every day she spoke to him on the 'phone the need grew stronger.

'If I asked, John might let me come back sooner,'

she suggested just two nights before she was due back. His reaction was disappointing.

'Patience love,' he said. 'Give me a chance to clear this backlog of work so that I can meet you at the airport the day after tomorrow. I want to be free to welcome you back properly.' His laugh was warm and wicked. 'And Fairlie—do you like diamonds?'

She was hot and cold at once, afraid to jump to this conclusion. Diamonds could be forever ... or they could be a gift from a man to his mistress.

'I don't know. Not always,' she said a little stiffly and he chuckled again.

'I thought a cluster of them in a ring—on your left hand. Would you like to choose a ring like that when you come back, Fairlie, my love?'

'Carson, are you proposing?' she squeaked.

'Yes and not doing a very good job of it. When you come back I'll do the whole bit—bended knee, bowed head—will you say "yes" to this question do you think?'

'Fool,' she managed huskily. 'Of course I'll say yes.'

That night she wrote to her father. 'Dear Dad,' she wrote, 'I love you ...' and after that the words just kept right on coming. He might never get the letter of course. He might move on before it reached him. But she posted it anyway on her way to the gallery in the morning. John Travis sold one of her exhibits that day while she stood by, glowing and barely able to keep her mind on the customer's conversation.

'My wife is crazy about it ...' the buyer told her and she smiled and graciously accepted a lot more praise. 'Got yourself a powerful sponsor,' he commented.

'Murchisons? I wouldn't know about powerful. But

I'm grateful to them. They've been extraordinarily generous.'

The man gave her an odd look. 'You know Murchisons is part of the Tate group don't you? Maybe you wouldn't,' he added on consideration. 'Tate's have nearly as many possessions as Adelaide Steamship. Most people have lost count.'

'Tate?' Fairlie's smile was wiped clean away. 'Are you sure?'

'My dear Miss Jones, I'm a broker. Of course I'm sure.'

It didn't necessarily mean anything, she kept telling herself—but Carson had just said yes when she asked if he knew of the company. Murchisons might have made the sponsorship decision quite independently . . . but why hadn't he said they were Tate owned? A cold pit yawned in the middle of her happiness. She skirted around the real question, not wanting to doubt—trying to trust—but she couldn't push away the picture that kept forming. She was here in Sydney—Nan was with the Reynolds. The house had been empty all week. No.

Using John's 'phone she called Carson's office. Sandra told her he was out but expected back later. Reluctantly, she rang Nan's house. And heard the chilling drone of a disconnected line. Even then she didn't want to admit the suspicion that lay waiting. The 'phone might be out of order, she told herself and stewed a little longer while the list of coincidences added up to the answer she dreaded. There were too many of them—far too many. She had to go home—to see Carson and Nan and Nan's house for herself.

In a matter of hours she was on a flight to Brisbane. She took a cab from the Airport and as it took her towards Kingsford Smith Drive a 727 took off, its noise ripping through the air. Fairlie didn't hear it. She heard instead the rumble and roar of big, orange machines. She shook her head faintly as the car crossed Breakfast Creek bridge and tried not to think of other broken promises, other betrayals.

'No.' She actually said the word aloud and the driver peered at her in the rear vision mirror. She took a deep breath and calmed herself. There was some very ordinary explanation for the generous sponsorship, the disconnected 'phone. A very ordinary down-to-earth answer . . .

There was.

'Here,' she said in a strangled voice and the cab stopped just down from the Colossus building. Cold spread through her in an instant ice age and Fairlie's heart contracted with the chill. Where Nan's house had stood was a barren waste. The garden, tended and watered for more than half a century was a ripped up series of channels criss-crossed with the grid marks of massive tyres. On a partly overturned clod clung a pathetic frond of fishbone fern. A very down-to-earth answer.

'Here love—you sure?'

In a flat, cold voice she said, 'No, sorry. Let me out further up will you at the Colossus building. And could you wait? I might be about ten minutes.'

Ten minutes—five—one. It wouldn't take long to say what she wanted. The numbness began to break up as she got in the lift and the pain started, crumpling her face and bowing her shoulders. At the tenth floor the hurt was cutting like a knife and she was fighting back. Eyes blue-green and hard as a turquoise seen by stormlight, she marched to the glass doors. 'Is he alone?' she asked Sandra and at the girl's doubtful 'Yes, but . . .' she opened Carson's door and went in, slamming it behind her. She leaned back against it.

'Fairlie——' Carson leapt from his chair, a smile on his lips. His hand was outstretched as he came to her but the cold in her eyes stopped him, stranding him on the pale tan sea of carpet.

'You bastard,' she said in a whisper that shouted around the office. 'You said you wouldn't do anything to hurt Nan.'

'Fairlie—it was meant to be——'

'A secret? A surprise?' she cut in. 'Well it damned well is a surprise. But it shouldn't be, should it Carson? You warned me you wanted the land—you never made any secret of that—you wanted me too and you didn't hide that either. And now you've conquered both. You must feel good.' She shoved her hands into her pockets, walked over to the architects model and gave a mirthless laugh. The tiny house had gone.

'You don't understand——'

'Oh I understand Carson. The whole thing was orchestrated with your superior talent for acquisition. And you said you would never be the man your father is!' He came to her then, took her arm and she flung it away as if a poisonous spider had settled on her.

'Farlie listen to me——'

But she didn't listen. 'You arranged to sponsor me through Murchisons——' His eyes narrowed. 'Yes, I found out about that today. You got me nicely out of the way, appealed to the artist in me—and the woman. Smooth, very smooth Carson. How naïve I was to suspect that you'd need to employ someone like James to distract me. Why if ever Lorelei ousts you from Colossus, you could always make a living as a gigolo to wealthy widows.'

His head went back at that. 'You said you trusted me.'

'Don't remind me,' she snapped. 'How long did you wait, Carson? Did you have Nan's signature before I'd even landed in Sydney?' She took several tight, raging steps away and turned back to him. 'You snake—you actually had the nerve to send "Nan's love" to me and I actually believed in you.'

'Not for long apparently,' he said.

'And I even started to believe in your beautifully portrayed eager lover image,' she forced herself to remember it—to hold it up and strip it of its magic. 'No wonder you came flying down to spend the night with me. You were paying for the room, paying for my exhibition. I didn't know it but I was a kept woman wasn't I, Carson—and a business man like you doesn't sponsor things for no return.' Her laugh was high—a detached, humourless sound that had its parallel keening cry inside her. 'Tell me, Carson, did I earn my keep? Did I turn out to be a sound investment? Was my performa——'

He strode to her and grabbed her shoulders. 'Shut up, Fairlie, you don't know what you're talking about. That night was something special and you know it.'

'Yes, it must have been okay. I was to get diamonds wasn't I? But the proposal—now *that* was a neat piece of ad-libbing to take my mind off coming back too soon. Hadn't you finished knocking down the house at the time?' She glared at him. 'You make an experienced lover, Carson, but don't count that night as a victory will you? I'll have forgotten you before I leave your high speed lift on the ground floor.'

'You won't forget,' he said between clenched teeth and hauled her close. 'That's your trouble. You can't forget and you can't forgive and you sure as hell can't trust. Your father doesn't even rate a letter from you because he left his grown up daughter—you broke your engagement because the man let you down. But you expected it to go wrong from the start. The poor guy didn't know did he, that whatever he did, he wouldn't measure up? Daddy had let down his little girl and so would every other man . . .'

He stopped because Fairlie's hand landed full on the side of his jaw.

'You don't like the truth, Fairlie?'

'What would you know about the truth?' she almost shouted, hurting unbearably at the approaching end of it all. In a moment she would walk out of here and never see him again. Never . . .

His grey eyes roved her face. 'More than you think. But you'll have to find out for yourself . . .' He lifted her forward and upwards so that her heels left the floor and his mouth met hers in a kiss that was angry. And just for a moment she wondered why he should be angry at all when he had won. But that empty allotment made a vivid picture behind her closed eyes and her own feelings swamped her. There was a larger, looming emptiness inside her. Carson had destroyed more than Nan's house.

'That's more like it, Carson,' she gasped when he let her go. 'The real you. Greedy and acquisitive. I just hope your ex-wife comes back early and removes David before it's too late for him.'

His fingers bit deeply into her upper arms at that, then he walked away.

'Where is she—Nan?'

He went to his desk and sat down. 'I'll give you her address,' he said and pulled a memo pad towards him and scrawled on it. He ripped the page from the others with a snap that sounded a final note in the hush. One of his 'phones began to ring but he ignored it, pushed the piece of paper across the desk. She walked over to take it.

'A nice rest home for the aged I suppose,' she said icily, reading the address. 'Or is it a flat?'

He didn't answer.

'Shall I give Nan your "love"?' she mocked.

CHAPTER TEN

SHE began to give Nan's new address to the taxi driver but she was crying and knew that she couldn't go to Nan yet. She had to pull herself together first. In a moment of complete desolation she realised she had nowhere to go. Nan's home had been hers too. She didn't even know where her car was. Gulping, she put on her dark glasses and gave the only address she could. The cab set her down ten minutes later outside Van Lewin's Gallery.

Pieter was in his office. 'Fairlie——' He beamed and came to her, arms outstretched. She dropped her bag and went to him blindly.

'Oh, Pieter . . .' She put her arms around his great girth and dropped her head on his shoulder. He stood still as a statue for a few moments then brought his arms around her—first one, then the other—gently, scarcely touching at first as if he feared he might crush her.

'Fairlie, darling——' he said in a strange tone and he lifted a hand to her hair. Pieter held her close, stroking her hair and murmuring something in Dutch. A sob jerked her body then another. He tensed.

'My sweet—what is it?'

'It's Carson.'

Pieter's arms tightened for one fierce moment. He sighed, muttered, 'Fool that I am. Carson. Of course it is Carson.' He led Fairlie to one of the two enormous wing backed chairs. 'Sit down and tell me what

Carson has done to make you run to Papa Pieter's arms, eh?'

She told him and he listened gravely.

'I'm sorry, Pieter, to come here like this, I've just left Carson's office and couldn't go to Nan in the state I was in. You see, I have no idea how she is feeling, whether Carson got her to sign something that she didn't know was important—or whether she let him persuade her to move willingly.'

'You think he is the kind of man who would do either of those things?'

'What else can I think?'

Pieter scooped back his blond hair, adjusted the collar of his shirt. 'Perhaps you are right my dear. Big business can be ruthless. I don't like to see you so distraught. But pehaps it is all for the best. See how you recovered from worthless Ben . . .'

She shook her head. 'This is different, Pieter.'

'You love Carson Tate?'

She nodded.

'But you thought you loved Ben, Fairlie, and you found out that you did not.'

'What I felt for Ben is nothing compared to this. That's why it hurts so to believe he would——' She snatched a tissue from her handbag and took off her sunglasses to dry her eyes.

Pieter levered himself from his chair. Once again he scooped back his hair with one large palm as he paced around his office, muttering in his native language.

'It is no good,' he said at last in English and hit his palms together. The robust slap brought Fairlie's head up. 'You must go to him. Now. Let him explain.'

'But Pieter—you said——'

Irritably he waved his hands. 'Never mind what I said. I am an old fool, deluding myself for a few minutes there that . . .' he hurried on, 'I have to stand by my original feelings about your Carson. He is a man I would trust. *You* must trust him. There must be an explanation for what he has done, for I do not think he would risk hurting you.'

She felt hope awaken. It was feeble, unjustified in the face of the facts as she knew them. Slowly she stood and raised her eyes to Pieter's. He wore a sad, weary look that penetrated her self-absorption. Swiftly he turned away and picked up his telephone.

'I'll arrange a cab for you, Fairlie. I would take you to him myself but a man can only be expected to do so much . . .' She blinked at that, a new suspicion blending with her confusion. 'Life is a big joke is it not, Fairlie?' Pieter had once said. But when he put the 'phone down he smiled in his usual way and asked her about the Sydney showing until the cab came.

He went outside with her and gave her bag to the driver who stowed it in the boot. Pieter opened the door for her. For the first time ever he kissed her on the mouth. Just for a few seconds he stayed close then he took a deep breath and moved away.

'Now go. I'm late for lunch and in some distress, my sweet.'

'Lunch? It's after three o'clock, Pieter,' she said in a voice that trembled.

'My dear, I've found this new French restaurant. Provincial cooking . . .' he put his fingertips to his mouth in Gallic approval, 'and the most *civilised* hours.'

He closed the door and she turned to raise her hand to him. But Pieter didn't wait to see her drive away.

She left her bag in the Colussus foyer with a surprised security guard and went up to Carson's floor. Sandra was quite passive and let her pass almost as if she had expected to see her again so soon. Carson's big desk was empty. He was on the glassed terrace, looking down at the wasteland where Nan's house had been. Fairlie watched him through the inner glass wall, loving every line of his body, remembering it, remembering how he had loved her with care and tenderness and passion. There had to be some extenuating circumstances. She couldn't think of even one as the automatic doors opened. At their swish Carson turned around. He didn't look surprised— standing there he would have seen her cab. His brows drew downwards and he watched her intently saying nothing.

'I didn't give you a chance to explain,' she began and when he merely narrowed his eyes, bowled on, 'though just what you can say to excuse *that* I can't imagine.' She flung out a hand at the empty ground below. Her eyes went to it and she gulped. 'You promised not to hurt her and you couldn't have bulldozed Nan's house without doing that.'

He said nothing but there was a new light deep in those watchful eyes. 'Aren't you going to say anything at all, Carson?' she cried. 'Tell me something to make me understand, damn you. Tell me it wasn't *you*. Tell me it was an earthquake, tell me it was white ants—*say* something.'

'Why?'

'Why?' she shrieked. 'Because I love you that's why and I don't want to believe that you would——' She lost the words because he grabbed her wrist and pulled her to him.

'Thank God for that,' he snarled down at her and she winced at his grip. 'Let's go.' He was striding, dragging her along with him. The glass doors shooshed open and closed. Across his lush carpeted office plaza he took her, pausing only to wrench his jacket from a built-in cupboard and his keys from his desk drawer. He didn't let go of her wrist. As they went out, his 'phone was ringing and the clothes hanger was rocking in the cupboard.

'Cancel that meeting with Erikson,' Carson said to Sandra.

'I already have,' she murmured to his back.

'Where are we going?' Fairlie said breathlessly in the lift. Carson pulled on his jacket and yanked her into his arms. He put his mouth on hers and kissed her punishingly all the way to the basement, containing her struggles without much trouble. With perfect timing he put her aside, holding on to her wrist just before the lift stopped.

'To see Nan,' he grated, and she was hurrying, more breathless than ever, taking two steps to his one as he dragged her along to his car. Her small dose of hope grew at his grim certainty. His manner seemed to be that of a man who expected to be vindicated. Nan must have gone willingly, then. The Rolls rushed out into the street, headlong as any sports car.

'I suppose Nan will tell me that she sold out to you because she liked you so much——'

'Be quiet.'

'I will not,' she said hotly, her head dizzy with conflicting emotions. Somewhere in her buzzing brain was something sensible, something about Nan talking on the 'phone to her that needed consideration, but she couldn't grasp it. 'What happened, did you ask her——'

'Shut up,' he thundered. 'I swear, Fairlie, if you say another word I'll stop the car and make you sorry.'

'I'm already sorry——'

He turned such a blazing look on her that she flinched back against the door. His hands gripped the steering wheel murderously and she looked from them to his face. She slid a hand to her throat.

'Exactly,' he clipped. 'Right now, it would give me great pleasure.'

The drive took around twenty minutes. The traffic was heavy and Carson swore a few times, throwing the dignified Rolls into tiny gaps that opened up respectfully for him. Off the main road he turned into a street of old houses on gracious allotments. Trees that had suffered no more than an occasional lopping for thirty or forty years, spread patches of shade over front gardens and footpaths. At least it was a peaceful area. But how would Nan get used to living in a flat or a retirement unit? The car slowed and parked behind two utility trucks laden with tools and ladders.

'Where is the place? I can't see any——' 'Flats,' she was going to say only it stuck in her throat. Overalled men were busy on the nearest house—pointing up brick work that looked new, painting weatherboards that had seen more than fifty years of Queensland sun. The house was cosy, small—only three new steps above the ground. It had a whimsical rotunda-shaped side to its verandah and a pleased look about it in spite of its battle-scarred appearance. Some ragged clumps of marguerite daisies bloomed pink along the trampled frontage where giant tyre marks were embedded in the ground.

'Nan's house——' she managed at last and turned to Carson. His face was tight as if he was grinding his teeth. He got out and came around to fling her door open, not offering a hand to help her scramble out on to the sloping grass verge.

'You *moved* it! Carson, why didn't you say?'

He strode away and left her standing there staring at Nan's house. He'd *moved* it! Tears rushed down her face. Fiercely she brushed them away. There were people blurred by the house. Carson talking to David who had a wheelbarrow full of pots. Nan pointed to a freshly dug flower bed and the boy halted the barrow beside it. Carson had found the solution. And this was his surpise for her.

'Fairlie——' Nan cried, as she hurried over to kiss her. 'Why did you have to come back early? Carson had such a surprise party planned for you.'

'Did he?' she croaked.

'It's been such a rush. Carson has had people working on it night and day. It usually takes ages you know, moving a house and making all the alterations to suit the council's notions of safety and so on. But he was so determined to have it all done, at least on the outside, before you got back.'

'Carson always moves fast,' she said huskily.

'And now you've come back early,' Nan sighed, 'and spoiled the surprise.'

'Yes. I spoiled it all right.'

The land belonged to the retired couple next door, Nan explained, then they'd decided to subdivide because a double allotment was too much work. It had been on the market for ages. Carson had had agents finding a suitable block of land from the moment he got the idea of moving the house.

'The former owners are so nice,' Nan exclaimed. 'Look at all the cuttings Mr Swain gave me for the garden . . .'

But it had only been six days, Fairlie thought.

'. . . and of course there are roses and the fruit trees they planted years ago . . .'

Carson must have brought every bit of his power

into play to get the land, move the house, and get it to this stage in six days.

'. . . oranges, dear—I can make marmalade . . .'

Even for him this must have been near impossible.

'We'll be able to move in in a week or so. I'm staying with the Reynolds. Carson has you booked in at a hotel—you don't mind do you? Oh *what* a shame about Carson's surprise party! He was planning to have lanterns and everything and a barbecue outside—a sort of homecoming for you and the house . . .'

Why hadn't she stopped to think? Nan had sounded so happy on the 'phone—so excited. And she would have rung her at the hotel had anything awful happened.

Lanterns, Nan's house magically removed to an idyllic setting. Carson's problem and Nan's solved to mutual satisfaction—and he had wanted to present her with the whole thing—*fait accompli*. She felt like laughing and crying, all at once.

'. . . and of course, the steps were getting too much for me, so Carson thought lowering the house would be ideal . . .'

It was such a touching, boyish use of his power. This gift to her had been stage managed and Carson no doubt had pictured the whole thing—her arrival from Sydney, her quick melt into his arms, her laughing curiosity as he drove her here instead of to the old, lonely site of Nan's house. Her gasp of delight when she saw what he had done and how perfect it was.

'. . . and the sun is on the clothes line all day . . .'

This was another side of Carson, another side of him to love when already she had found so much. And she had turned all his plans against him, called him names.

'Gee, Fairlie, it would have been fun if you hadn't come back. We were going to have a party. Me and Dad were going to put up some streamers——'

'Oh—well—I'm sorry, David.'

But she was looking at Carson who had taken Nan aside. He threw her a glance rather reminiscent of his son in one of his sulks, then walked away to speak to a painter.

'Come and meet my neighbours,' Nan said a few minutes later. Her eyes were sparkling, her cheeks pink as the marguerite daisies. Fairlie was taken away to meet the Swains. Carson must have auditioned them for the role of Nan's neighbours she thought. They were nigh on perfect.

When they came back to the house the workmen had gone. So had David. And Carson.

'I expect he's just driving David over to Alex's house. He's staying overnight. They're working on Alex's brother's car now that yours is finished.'

A taxi pulled up and tooted its horn. Nan dashed into the empty house and fetched her bag. She gave Fairlie the front door key.

'You won't mind locking up will you, dear? That's my cab to take me to the Reynolds. Carson arranged for one to call by each day when I've finished pottering in the garden.' She kissed Fairlie and went down the three new steps with a sigh of contentment.

'But Nan—what about me?'

Nan looked back from the lawn. 'It wasn't a bit premature letting him call me Nan,' she said almost to herself, her eyes lingering with pleasure on her house. She looked again at Fairlie. 'If you wait, my dear—Carson will come for you.'

The taxi drove away. Fairlie twirled the key on its string and stood on Nan's verandah. Carson will come for you . . . after a while she smiled and sat on the top step. Mr Carson Tate was stage managing events again. This time she would wait her cue. It was a long time coming but Fairlie leaned against the verandah post and took her punishment.

The sun went down and the clouding sky was washed with its leftover colour. A plover flew over, its scolding cry sharp in the quiet. Somewhere a dog barked. Still she sat and waited. The Rolls made scarcely a sound as it pulled up. Fairlie watched Carson get out and walk towards her in the deepening twilight.

'About time,' she said when he was at the foot of the steps looking up.

'I hope you thought I wasn't coming.'

'Never crossed my mind.'

'Pity,' he observed. 'I should have kept you waiting here until midnight.'

'Why didn't you?'

He came up the steps and pulled her to her feet. 'Never mind. Give me the key. I'll lock up.' He took it and went into the dark house then reappeared a few moments later to lock the front door. 'Let's go.'

The big car moved off at its own dignified pace. No impassioned rushes and screeches this time.

'You were right,' Fairlie said. 'I expected the worst because I'd been let down before. I'm sorry.'

He grunted.

'I wrote to my father,' she said lightly. 'After all this time.'

'When did you do that?'

'After you came to see me in Sydney.'

This time he didn't answer at all but his silence had a certain satisfaction about it.

In the apartments' car park, he threw her a brooding look and got her suitcase out of the boot.

'I'd forgotten that,' she said a little huskily. 'How did you know I'd left it at Colossus?'

'The security officer brought it up. He, like everyone else in my offices, seemed to know who you were. And he also seemed to assume I'd be personally interested in your luggage.'

'Was that embarrassing for you? In your position I mean?'

As they left the elevator he gave a snort. 'What's a little more embarrassment? Since you came to live with your grandmother you've driven the machinery, burst into my offices, beat your fists on the foyer doors late at night and been seen leaving my office with your blouse wet. My reputation has been through the shredder. Embarrassment!' he hooted.

'I've been a nuisance, haven't I, Carson?' she said in a meek voice.

'Yes.' He shut the apartment door and dropped her suitcase. 'You've been a bloody nuisance from the moment I set eyes on you. Come here,' he added thickly and pulled her into his arms. His kiss was hard and brief. A rebuke. 'You drive me insane——' he said raggedly and kissed her again, this time with hunger, need. And love. Gentler now, he held her, moving his hands over her back, stroking her hair, her face. Fairlie rested against him, in a blaze of joy to have him close.

'Carson, I said some terrible things to you.'

'Names I can live with.'

'—I said you were greedy and acquisitive and a snake——'

'Sticks and stones.'

'—and, and I said you could earn a living as a gigolo——'

'At my age that's a compliment.'

'—that you were a bad influence on David.'

'I didn't believe that.' He waited a moment then held her at arm's length. 'And——?' he prompted.

'Surely that was all?'

'You told me you'd forget me before you left the elevator on the ground floor. Now *that* I didn't like.' He brought her close again, touched his mouth to hers. 'I didn't like that at all.'

'I couldn't forget you if I spent a year in an elevator.'

'A year?' he protested.

'All right then—ten years—a lifetime——'

'That's better.' He kissed her again. And this time it was all love.

'Can you forgive me for ruining your surprise—for doubting you?'

'I guess I'll have to. How come you took so long to come back after you'd bawled me out?'

She hesitated, reluctant to speak of Pieter. 'When I left you I was so desolate that I went to Pieter's gallery. He—calmed me down, made me see that I hadn't given you a chance to explain—hadn't given myself a chance to trust you ...' But he had been tempted to drive a wedge between her and Carson—a wedge that couldn't have survived once she'd seen Nan's house but Pieter hadn't known that.

'He cares for you,' Carson said. 'I think he guessed how it would be between us that night at Nan's place. He's a gentleman but how he wanted to put me down.'

'And you let him a few times, didn't you?'

'I could afford to be generous even then.'

'I'm very fond of him,' Fairlie said sadly, thinking that those comical scenes she had played with the big man had had, after all, a little truth in them.

'I can feel for the man—sending you to me——'

'I'd like to think I would have gone back anyway—before I saw the house. Carson, I really am so sorry. When one of John's customers told me that Murchisons was part of the Tate group, I tried not to be suspicious but I'd got used to suspecting—and then, when the house was gone——'

'So that's how you found out. I picked Murchisons because they're so obscure to most people. If you found out I was behind it I knew you'd get your independent hackles up and accuse me of patronage but I didn't think you'd see it as sinister.'

'Why did you sponsor me?'

Letting her go, he shrugged off his jacket. 'A self-indulgent thing. I was crazy about you by then and got a kick out of doing something that would please you. But it was sheer coincidence that your Sydney trip occurred about the time I confirmed it was a proposition to move the house. Nan said something some time ago that made me realise it was only the house itself and not the actual *location* she couldn't give up. But I didn't say anything in case it wasn't practical. It seemed such a perfect solution that I suppose I didn't really believe it would be possible. I had to get a man in to look around and confirm that the house could be moved. Hell, I was certain you'd find him there checking the beams and raise Cain like you did over the surveyors.'

'I would have,' she grinned. 'Didn't Nan see him?'

'Yes. I told her he was checking the wiring because of a council regulation.'

'She didn't mention it.'

'That's because she trusts me.'

'Nan's a very smart lady,' she said softly, 'I wish I'd heeded her.'

Carson sighed. 'So do I my love. So do I.' He

opened the door on to the rooftop terrace and with an arm about her waist, led her out into the cool, evening air. It was dark now. The river glittered with reflected lights along the bank. A boat slid by, just a yellow patch and a few beads of light in the darkness. Above, the sky was full of cloud, empty of stars.

'Marry me soon, Fairlie.'

'Tomorrow if you like.'

'Would you?' he chuckled.

'Just give me time to buy a wedding dress.'

'What—no suit and tie?'

'Not for this occasion,' she laughed, 'Carson, what about David? Shouldn't we give him time to adjust to the idea?'

'David knows how I feel about you. I told him. Every night you were away I was pacing around until he asked me what was the matter. He didn't say much but I think he was quite pleased.' He paused. 'Fairlie——'

'Oh yes, definitely.'

'Definitely—what?'

'I'd love to have David living with us—if you think he might want to.'

He turned her into his arms with a sigh. 'Are you always going to read my mind you witch?'

'Not always. I wouldn't want to get bored,' she said pertly.

'Bored!' He pulled her tight against him. 'You won't get bored reading my mind, lover, I'll make sure of that——' He kissed her thoroughly, holding her, touching her to show her how exciting mind-reading could be.

'I see what you mean,' she giggled, 'but maybe after a while even *that* could be boring ... say, twenty years.'

'Say thirty, forty,' he corrected. 'This is for keeps, Fairlie.' Suddenly he was serious. 'I mean it. I've made some stupid mistakes and I won't make those again. I might even let Lorelei have Colossus one day if it starts to take over our lives. But I can't guarantee that I won't make other mistakes.'

'I'm not asking for guarantees,' she said softly. 'Or for every minute of your time. Just your love. Anyway, I can't guarantee that I'll make a good wife. In fact, now that I come to think of it I probably won't. My cooking isn't very good. Nothing like Mrs Strachan's and I hope you don't think that Nan's date loaf runs in the family.'

He groaned. 'You can't make prize-winning date loaf?'

'Heavy, soggy things,' she said gloomily.

'How about knitting——?'

'Terrible. Slow as a wet week and lousy tension. But don't worry, we'll get Nan to knit our baby clothes.'

'Ms Fairlie Jones—wanting babies?' he teased.

'Mrs Fairlie Tate wanting babies,' she said. 'Though I daresay that's all old hat to you.'

'Was that what you were thinking at the hospital when I was reminiscing over David's birth?'

'Yes—I suppose I was jealous that you'd had all that with someone else.'

'We have it all ahead of us. And it won't be old hat, I promise you. Our own miracle. Two miracles, I think. A girl would be nice first, then a boy——'

'Oh, I see, you've already drawn up plans——'

'I'll need help,' he admitted, and nuzzled her neck. 'A certain amount of co-operation on these kinds of projects is—ouch!' He drew back, rubbing his ear where her teeth had nipped him. 'I'll probably be sorry. If our kids turn out like you my life will be one long farce. In later years when you've mellowed I'll tell them that it all started when their staid, placid mother jumped aboard an earthmover on a Colossus site——'

'Forget it.'

'It's true.'

'Forget the staid, placid bit. I've no intention of ever being either.'

Carson's eyes gleamed. 'That's a promise?'

'A promise. But your family might not approve——'

'They'll love you. They'd better.'

'—might not approve of a woman who will probably spend a great deal of time in paint-spattered overalls— because I warn you, our two miracles notwithstanding, I intend to do a lot of painting.'

'I'll pose for you,' he said complacently. 'As often as you like.'

'Rash.'

'Utterly reckless.' He laid his cheek against her hair. 'I love you.'

Fairlie smiled and looked up at the clouded sky.

'Well——?' he prompted. 'Isn't there something you want to tell *me*?'

'There are no stars tonight . . .' she said dreamily.

He laughed. 'There will be.' Carson hooked his arm in hers and drew her inside. 'Now what did you want to tell me?'

'Oh, didn't I say, Carson love? I love you. Madly. Forever.'

'That's better. But I won't be happy until I have our marriage certificate in my hands.'

'Why's that?'

'My darling girl, you know how I work. I always get it in writing.'

Coming Next Month in Harlequin Presents!

WORLDWIDE LIBRARY IS YOUR TICKET TO ROMANCE, ADVENTURE AND EXCITEMENT

Experience it all in these big, bold Bestsellers— Yours exclusively from WORLDWIDE LIBRARY WHILE QUANTITIES LAST

To receive these Bestsellers, complete the order form, detach and send together with your check or money order (include 75¢ postage and handling), payable to WORLDWIDE LIBRARY, to:

In the U.S.
WORLDWIDE LIBRARY
Box 52040
Phoenix, AZ
85072-2040

In Canada
WORLDWIDE LIBRARY
P.O. Box 2800, 5170 Yonge Street
Postal Station A, Willowdale, Ontario
M2N 6J3

Quant.	Title	Price
_____	WILD CONCERTO, Anne Mather	$2.95
_____	A VIOLATION, Charlotte Lamb	$3.50
_____	SECRETS, Sheila Holland	$3.50
_____	SWEET MEMORIES, LaVyrle Spencer	$3.50
_____	FLORA, Anne Weale	$3.50
_____	SUMMER'S AWAKENING, Anne Weale	$3.50
_____	FINGER PRINTS, Barbara Delinsky	$3.50
_____	DREAMWEAVER, Felicia Gallant/Rebecca Flanders	$3.50
_____	EYE OF THE STORM, Maura Seger	$3.50
_____	HIDDEN IN THE FLAME, Anne Mather	$3.50
_____	ECHO OF THUNDER, Maura Seger	$3.95
_____	DREAM OF DARKNESS, Jocelyn Haley	$3.95

	YOUR ORDER TOTAL	$_____
	New York and Arizona residents add appropriate sales tax	$_____
	Postage and Handling	$ .75
	I enclose	$_____

NAME _____

ADDRESS _____ APT.# _____

CITY _____

STATE/PROV. _____ ZIP/POSTAL CODE _____
WW3

What the press says about Harlequin romance fiction...

"When it comes to romantic novels...
Harlequin is the indisputable king."
— *New York Times*

"...always with an upbeat, happy ending."
— *San Francisco Chronicle*

"Women have come to trust these
stories about contemporary people,
set in exciting foreign places."
— *Best Sellers*, New York

"The most popular reading matter of
American women today."
— *Detroit News*

"...a work of art."
— *Globe & Mail*, Toronto

Can you keep a secret?

You can keep this one plus 4 free novels